FOREVER MY QUEEN...

"YOU GIVE A BEAUTY-QUEEN-SMILE and they get a picture for the yearbook, and everyone feels more comfortable," she continued. "Safe. *That's* the service we do for the people of Golem Creek—the other kids at Honorius High. Our fucking big-toothed-bullshit-empty-eyed smiles make them feel like everything is safe. *We* have those dreams so that *they* can sleep at night. Our smiles maintain the pretense that evil isn't real. And it's bullshit. It's all bullshit. But we do it. Isobel and I have done it for years—you're going to do it *once*. So yeah, it sucks. But you figure out a way to deal. We accept whatever bullshit crowns and flowers or whatever it is that they give us. And we smile. And then after the dance the three of us will come back to my house and we will figure all this out, okay?"

RED HOT HEX MAGICK

The Witches of Golem Creek
Book I

Nadia Xavier

FOURTH MANSIONS PRESS

The Witches of Golem Creek
Book I
RED HOT HEX MAGICK

FOURTH MANSIONS PRESS, LLC
Charlottesville, Virginia

fourthmansions.com

ISBN: 978-0-578-51993-7

Cover art and title page illustration © 2019 Chris Claxton

Cover design by Chris Claxton & Fourth Mansions Press, LLC

For Helen Vaughan,
with her companions in the world
beyond the shadows.

I

It was exactly one week since Morgan Firestone last had The Dream. And she wasn't keen on having another. For a full three days afterward she kept her boyfriend Zach on the phone with her until she fell asleep. He didn't know about The Dream, of course, and even if he did he wouldn't care. "Dreams don't mean anything, babe," she could hear him saying. "So what?"

Zach wasn't the superstitious type—Morgan liked that about him. Every night that week she'd repeated the same mantra as she brushed her long chestnut hair in front of the mirror before bed: "It was just a dream." But there was still something about it that she couldn't shake. Something about the hazy-yet-all-too-clear incantations that had reverberated through her mind even after waking. The images of the other women in the circle—unkempt, wild-eyed. And the fact that she woke up with dirt crusted under her freshly-manicured fingernails.

But after a week of uneasy but thankfully dream-less sleep, Morgan felt confident that it had, in fact, only been a dream.

The week of the dream, Morgan had other things to worry about: a mani-pedi before the homecoming party on Saturday, coaxing her History teacher into bumping that C+ on the last exam up to a B, figuring out a way to get out of the weekly obligatory therapy session, and making Danielle Rider regret the day she first set foot in Golem Creek.

Morgan wasn't a bad person. It was Danielle who started everything. And Morgan had tried—really *tried*—to make her feel at home those first few weeks. They'd even become friends, skipping sixth period to take Morgan's Mustang GT to the mall, spending long afternoons lounging in the pool and even longer evenings with Morgan's group drinking vodka out of the back of Taylor Johnson's matte-black Mercedes in the parking lot of the abandoned bank off Memorial. Danielle fit in perfectly—too perfectly, though. And definitely too fast. And it was only one month after her arrival that Danielle broke Morgan's cardinal rule: *don't go after Giles Levi.*

Not that Danielle knew this was Morgan's rule. All Danielle knew was that Morgan was happily dating Zach Corey, and had been for some time. Nobody, in fact, knew that Morgan and Giles had been hooking up since freshman year—and certainly no one suspected that Isobel and Giles had gotten together roughly around the same time. But it was an unspoken rule among Morgan's clique that Giles was strictly off limits. The day after the senior trip to the waterpark, and the day before the night of The Dream, the hallways of Honorius High were buzzing with the titillating stories of Dani and Giles's infamous liplock at the top of the Wet-n-Wild. It was, as Morgan's best friend Isobel put it, "a fucking disaster."

"Why?" Cynthia Wildes asked that afternoon as the group crowded around a mirror in the second-floor bathroom.

"Because," Isobel ventured slowly, catching

Morgan's eye in the mirror. "We don't need more bad publicity about the girls in this group being fucking sluts."

"Bad publicity?" scoffed Emma Martin. "You sound like your dad."

Morgan turned from the mirror and glared daggers at Emma.

"You *know* we don't talk about Izzy's dad. Besides, so what if she does? This group could learn a thing or two about good PR after what happened at last year's formal." Morgan paused to drop the tube of lip gloss in her purse and let the very-real quilted Chanel bag click loudly shut. "Emma."

Blushing, Emma tried to turn away from Morgan but found that she couldn't.

"You know what I mean—"

"Whatever," Isobel interrupted, rolling her eyes. Morgan turned her attention to the mirror once more, releasing Emma from her gaze, and met her own reflection squarely in the eyes. She paused for a moment, as if looking for something in the reflected image and not finding it, before turning back to the group.

"But come on, girls," Morgan said, her tight smile varnished with Dior lip glow. "Let's not slut-shame. She may be new here, but Dani is our friend. We have no idea what was going on in her head—if any of this is actually true."

Cynthia and Emma both shrugged and, closing their respective (knock-off) Chanel bags, started up a conversation about the latest Ryan Carpenter movie as they walked out of the bathroom. Isobel moved to follow, but Morgan grabbed her arm, digging her nails into Isobel's skin.

"What the—" Isobel tried to jerk her arm away from Morgan's grasp but found that she couldn't.

"We've got a problem," Morgan whispered.

"I'm aware," Isobel hissed back.

"Do you have a plan?"

"Did I *make* a plan since we heard about this an hour ago? Oh, yeah. Sure." Isobel tried again to break free from Morgan's hold, but Morgan only dug her fingernails in deeper. "Obviously not. Jesus fucking *Christ*—let *go*! You're hurting me."

Morgan let go of Isobel's arm. She hadn't realized she was holding on so hard, but didn't want to lose face.

"Yeah. Well—remember that."

Isobel rolled her eyes, unfazed. "Whatever."

The bathroom door opened and another girl rushed in as the late bell rang for third period. The girl stopped in her tracks when she saw Morgan Firestone and Isobel Gowdie standing there, evidently in some sort of argument.

"Oh—sorry..." she muttered before rushing off. Morgan glared at the space where the girl had stood before turning back to Isobel.

"Ditch fourth period and meet me in the woods so we can talk about this in private," Morgan commanded. "The Spot—you know."

Isobel was already halfway out the door, her blonde hair swinging as she walked.

"Fine."

Finally alone, Morgan turned back to the mirror and met her own eyes again. A fucking disaster, indeed.

II

THE SPOT WAS A secret campground in the woods behind the school that Morgan and her clique used for various, often illegal, purposes. It was just close enough to the school to serve as the perfect location for a midday hook-up, shot, or toke, but far enough away to never arouse suspicion from the school. In fact, it was almost as if when you were at The Spot you were cloaked in invisibility. No one—school security, cops, kids, hikers—ever seemed to stumble across The Spot. Most of the group, if they ever thought about it, chalked it up to teenage luck, but Morgan and Isobel knew the truth.

It was Giles Levi who first found The Spot. Or The Spot found him, Morgan was never sure. It was also where Giles brought Morgan the night of the first hook-up—and later (or earlier, Morgan was never clear on the exact timeline) where Giles brought Isobel.

Isobel reached for the already-open bottle of red wine wedged in the gnarled roots of the biggest tree, pulled out the cork with her teeth, and took a long drink.

"We don't know that he fucked her." She took another drink. "Yet."

Morgan laughed bitterly.

"Um, this is Giles we're talking about. We know." Morgan reached over and took the wine from Isobel. "We know he needs a third. The timing, everything...

just. Goddamn it. I've been doing everything in my power to keep all those stupid, ungrateful bitches at this school safe from that…"

Isobel grabbed the bottle back and took a drink.

"You? All you, huh?"

Morgan rolled her eyes.

"Jesus Christ, Isobel. Yes, me—and you. Thank you."

"Thank you," Isobel mumbled, leaning back against the tree trunk and closing her eyes. "Shit. We are so fucked."

"Maybe not. Maybe… You said it yourself. Maybe they didn't do anything. Maybe it's all a rumor."

"Morgan, I saw it," Isobel said firmly.

"You weren't even *there*! You—"

"You know what I mean. I saw it."

"Maybe there's still time," Morgan ventured, trying to convince herself more than Isobel. "The full moon is tonight. If they didn't do anything yet, maybe there's still time."

"Maybe," Isobel said, taking another long swig from the wine bottle. Morgan glanced down at her fingernails, feigning nonchalance.

"So that's still happening, huh?"

"What?"

"Seeing things…you know, visions or whatever."

Isobel sighed, irritated.

"I just told you."

"Right," Morgan mumbled as she took the bottle from Isobel.

"What about you? Noticing anything weird?"

"I don't know…" Morgan lied. "Nothing out of the ordinary."

Lifting the bottle to her lips, Morgan shrugged, hoping her friend hadn't registered the incident in the bathroom that morning when she'd effectively immobilized both Emma and Isobel with a glance. In fact, Morgan had been noticing things like that happening more and more over the past few weeks. She'd always held a particular sway over people. But lately it seemed as if her power was growing in a way she didn't quite understand. It made her feel uneasy—but also, if she was being honest with herself, really damn good.

Isobel took back the bottle and let out a quick laugh.

"Looks like we killed it."

Morgan turned toward her friend, startled, snapping out of her thoughts.

"What?"

"The bottle," Isobel laughed, turning the empty wine bottle over so the final red drops of drugstore pinot noir dripped slowly onto the forest floor like watery blood. "Looks like we killed it."

Morgan straightened herself up and fished in her purse for a stick of gum.

"Killed it," she muttered. "Right."

III

MORGAN AND ISOBEL BARELY spoke on the walk back to the school from The Spot. They hadn't exactly outlined a plan for confronting Dani, but Morgan was feeling confident that her ever-increasing persuasive abilities would pretty much take care of things for them. Morgan and Isobel had racked up quite a bit of practice intimidating girls at Honorius High over the past four years. The other girls at school simply regarded this as typical queen-bee-rich-bitch behavior, and Morgan felt secretly bitter that no one would ever know enough to appreciate the service she and Isobel were offering by keeping the Honorius girls in line and, most importantly, safe.

Both girls expected the usual amount of drama in their dealings with Dani later that afternoon. They were experts in the art of girl-on-girl intimidation. Passive-aggressive at first—little hints about Giles and his reputation, maybe a vague allusion to an unnamed STD or something; they could get creative in the moment, improvise a little—moving on to *aggressive*-aggressive if she didn't cave. Various threats about her future standing in the group, potential rumors that might be spread, etc. Usually the passive-aggressive approach was successful. High school girls responded well to psychological intimidation. The whole process was so routine it had become boring.

What neither girl expected was to run into Giles

just as they were exiting the woods.

Giles Levi wasn't handsome in the Zach Corey kind of way. Zach was a safe kind of handsome—clean-cut, simple, easy. The kind of on-brand high school attractiveness that, if Morgan was being honest, wasn't actually handsome at all. Not like Giles, who exuded a distinctive troubled-movie-star quality that was simultaneously attractive and repulsive all at once.

"Fuck," Isobel muttered as soon as she caught sight of Giles's black leather jacket. She grabbed Morgan's hand and squeezed. "He's such a goddamn cliché in that stupid jacket. It's like he literally learned how to be a teenager by watching old James Dean movies."

Morgan bit her lip to keep from laughing.

"I'm pretty sure he did."

Giles was leaning against a tree at the edge of the woods with a half-smoked cigarette hanging out of his mouth.

"Now or never," Isobel sighed as they approached. Giles, hearing the sound of their footsteps on the crackling leaves of the forest floor, moved to turn around. The girls dropped their hands and girded themselves for the impending conversation.

"Hey," Morgan said flatly, tossing her glossy hair over her shoulder.

"Hey, Morgan," Giles smiled, tossing his cigarette into the dirt. "Isobel," he added, casting his black gaze in Isobel's direction.

"What's been going on?" Morgan asked, wondering if he could hear her heartbeat.

"Oh, you know..." he trailed off, grinning.

Evasive, Morgan thought. Fuck him.

"Come on, man," Isobel suddenly blurted out. "Is it true or what?"

Giles raised an eyebrow.

"What?"

"Oh my god, you fucking asshole," Isobel growled. "Dani. You finally found your third, huh?"

"I have no idea what you're talking about, Isobel. And, as usual, your obsession with proclaiming your distaste for me has utterly clouded your ability to communicate properly."

Isobel was seething.

"You know, Giles," Morgan answered for Isobel, "we've managed to keep a lid on things here. I thought Isobel and I had been pretty good about keeping things...keeping you, or him"—she glanced around the edge of the woods and quickly toward the school to make sure no one else was approaching who might overhear their conversation—"satisfied, or whatever. It was supposed to end with us."

Giles laughed, lighting another cigarette.

"Don't try to rewrite history, Morgan. It's insulting. I'm not stupid. And neither are you—either of you," he grinned at Isobel. "I'm honestly surprised by your reactions. I told you from day one—*day one*—that I needed a third. And yes, you girls have been excellent companions these past four years and we genuinely appreciate that so much. But you knew this was coming. This was all part of the deal that *you*"—he gestured toward both girls with the cigarette, smoke billowing from his fingers towards their faces—"*both* of you made."

Isobel lurched forward as if she was going to hit

Giles.

"*You—*"

Giles laughed and backed up quickly, holding his hands out in mock defense.

"Hey, don't be mad at me, okay? Besides, you girls have no idea what's coming to you out of all this. You think you made some deal with me for popularity in high school? Please—this is just the beginning. I know you've noticed your powers growing—both of you." Giles took a drag on his cigarette and looked directly at Morgan. "Even if you just lied to Isobel about it back at The Spot a few minutes ago."

Isobel, glaring furiously at both Giles and Morgan, opened her mouth to speak, but was cut off by the sound of someone approaching from the football field.

"Hey!"

The friendly voice cut through the tension as Zach jogged over to the group.

"Hey, Zach," Morgan smiled at her boyfriend, regaining her composure.

Giles nodded in Zach's direction, tossing his second cigarette into the dirt. Isobel, still seething, crossed her arms in front of her chest.

"Bad day, Isobel?" Zach asked.

"A fucking disaster," she replied through her teeth.

"Bummer."

"What are you up to, Zach?" Morgan asked, popping another piece of gum in her mouth to hide the scent of the red wine. Zach grinned and threw his arm around Giles's shoulders.

"We were going to head out to The Spot...you

know, 4:20 or whatever..."

"It's noon," Isobel replied.

"Aw, yeah...well, you know how it is..." Zach laughed.

"Right."

Giles patted Zach on the shoulder and smiled broadly at both girls, his eyes shifting from black back to light brown.

"Ladies, if you'll excuse us..."

"Later!" Zach called out as Giles steered him into the woods.

Morgan and Isobel watched as the reddening foliage seemed to close in, somehow camouflaging Giles and Zach as they made their way deeper into the forest. Morgan never got used to that sight. It was as if the trees actually moved, closed in like curtains.

Morgan was still staring into the woods when she heard the pronouncement she knew was coming from Isobel:

"Fuck you, Morgan."

Turning, Morgan fixed Isobel with a furious stare. She could feel Isobel's fear as she held her in her gaze. This time she didn't need to use her fingernails.

"What—" Isobel tried to speak but found she couldn't.

Morgan maintained the stare, trying to enjoy the power she had over her friend—but realizing quickly that she could not. She just felt sick. She dropped her eyes, releasing Isobel. Isobel fell to her knees and let out a breath as if she'd been suffocating.

"What the *fuck* did you just do to me?"

"I don't know," Morgan replied. "That's the first

time I've tried to do it. Before it was just...happening. I don't know."

"So this is what's been going on?" Isobel asked, regaining her strength and standing up, brushing the dirt off her skirt. "I've got these visions, you've got this...power."

"Yeah."

Isobel nodded thoughtfully, taking it all in.

"Cool."

IV

MORGAN AND ISOBEL NEVER found Dani that day. They both asked around, searched the hallways, called her at home. Nobody knew where she was—no other students, no teachers, nobody. Dani had never been absent before, so her absence on that day was particularly unsettling. The strangest aspect of Dani's disappearance, however, was that all day people seemed to remember her as being there—well, *there*, but not *quite*. Morgan was getting seriously impatient as she went from teacher to teacher making up some excuse every time—Dani was her ride home, lab partner, etc.—only to hear the same thing: Dani was on the attendance sheet, but didn't turn in her daily assignment; Dani *wasn't* on the attendance sheet, but did turn in her homework. Other students remembered seeing Dani eating lunch in the cafeteria, studying during lunch in the library, and going off grounds for lunch at the mall food court. Dani had been both present and absent all day, and not even Morgan's icy gaze could get anyone to give her a straight answer. This, Morgan thought, did not bode well.

After school Morgan met back up with Isobel in the parking lot. Isobel was waiting, sitting on the hood of Morgan's car wearing black cat-eye sunglasses and filing her long red nails irritably.

"Any luck?" Morgan called out.

Isobel looked up and lowered the sunglasses to

meet Morgan's gaze.

"What do you think?"

"Yeah, same."

"What the hell?" Isobel asked, as both girls climbed into the car. "You think Giles is like...hiding her or something?"

Morgan pulled down the sun visor and checked her makeup in the mirror. Perfect.

"I don't know," she said as she flipped the visor back up. "Either that or...I mean, let's say she really didn't do anything. And Giles is just messing with us. Which he loves to do, as we both know. And she just...maybe someone, Emma or Cynthia or whoever, told her that I would be pissed and she bailed. Skipped school."

Isobel raised one perfectly arched eyebrow.

"Dani? Skip school?"

"I said I don't know, okay? But I don't want to jump to conclusions here. I'm freaking out, Izzy."

"I know," Isobel sighed. "What the fuck did Giles mean back there about 'growing powers'? Did he promise you—I mean, do you remember any..." she trailed off.

"We said we'd never talk about that," Morgan snapped.

"I know."

Morgan closed her eyes and took a few deep breaths. If there was one thing Morgan prided herself on it was her lack of vulnerability. But today was different, and even though she desperately didn't want to appear vulnerable in front of Isobel, at that moment it seemed that she had no choice.

"It's like a bad dream. I used to remember...I couldn't *not* think about it. But now—it's like it's so far away now." Someone in the parking lot laid on their horn, snapping Morgan out of the memory. "But no, I don't...I don't remember there being any strings or whatever. I thought it was a pretty simple exchange. And he said...I mean, yeah he said he needed a third but when things worked out so well I figured..." she trailed off.

"Yeah, me too," Isobel added. "We had the power. It worked."

"And then we have the power to keep that third girl from him."

"It was actually a pretty brilliant plan," Isobel laughed.

"Yeah," Morgan muttered.

"Or, it would have been if it had actually worked."

"And if he's got Dani then it didn't. And we're..."

"Fucked," Isobel finished.

"Yep."

Morgan felt frozen in her seat. Isobel rolled down the window and lit a cigarette from Morgan's secret stash in the glove compartment. The smell of the smoke was making Morgan feel sick, like she might vomit. It reminded her of that late summer night before freshman year—the night she first saw Giles Levi smoking outside the high school—the night she followed him back through the curtains of trees to The Spot where he told her he could make her greatest wish come true.

Morgan had never talked to Isobel about what happened at The Spot that night. Giles introduced them on the first day of school that year and they'd been inseparable ever since. Morgan knew Isobel had gone through the same initiation she had, but they never spoke about it—about the pain, the blood, the book—Giles standing there smoking, bored, leaning against a tree, and the hooved creature that hobbled out of a clearing, just enough pale moonlight cast on its gnarled features to reveal that it was monstrously ugly, and definitely not human.

Morgan never talked to anyone about that night, of course. How could she? Admit to her parents she'd sold her soul for the promise of four years guaranteed prom queen? Yeah, right. They'd have her put away or medicated out of her mind. So she found other things to talk about during her obligatory therapy sessions—the burdens of popularity, petty troubles with Zach, the isolation she felt from her absent, self-absorbed parents. But the memory was always there, seared in her mind like the scars on her and Isobel's hands...only it had grown distant. Over the years both girls had to keep up their visits regularly—that was part of the deal. But what was once so monstrous now seemed routine. And just like the power and popularity it bought her, sometimes it was a burden.

But sometimes she loved it.

"Hey," Isobel snapped her fingers in front of Morgan's face. "What do you think?"

"What?" Morgan asked, shaking herself out of her reverie.

"Dani's house. Should we go?"

"Oh, right," Morgan straightened her posture and put the keys in the ignition, starting the car. "We'll check on her there. And if she's not home..."

"We'll figure that out later," Isobel said wearily, tossing the cigarette into the parking lot and adjusting her sunglasses.

V

DANI LIVED AT THE edge of town in an area that neither Morgan nor Isobel would ever have deigned to visit otherwise. Dani's mother worked as a history professor at the university around the corner, but after the divorce, Dani explained, her mother's income had been swallowed up in legal fees. And although the university was nice, the area surrounding it was most definitely not. Morgan had only been here once before, to pick Dani up for a double date with Zach and his best friend Sam Proctor, and she wasn't exactly thrilled to be back. Tattered curtains, peeling paint, a broken porch swing. The house looked practically abandoned. Isobel lowered her sunglasses and gave the house a once-over.

"Well, this is just sad," she muttered to Morgan as they approached the front door. Overgrown weeds stretched across the concrete walkway, and the brown grass was nearly obscured by dead leaves.

"No kidding."

Morgan reached up for the brass doorknocker but was startled to see it was in the shape of a goat's head. Withdrawing her hand as if she'd been stung, she rapped with her knuckles on the peeling red wood instead.

Morgan and Isobel could hear someone approaching from inside the house, but whoever it was seemed to be taking an awfully long time. Isobel sighed and leaned toward the window, gazing over the tops of her sunglasses to peer into the dark house.

"I can't see anything," she mumbled. "Are you sure this is the right place?"

At that moment the door swung open, and a thin woman who strongly resembled Dani, with the same coffee-colored skin and perfect cheekbones, stood before them. The woman's hair was twisted into long and unkempt dreadlocks, her clothes were wrinkled, and she had dark circles under her hazel eyes.

"Can I help you?" the woman asked cautiously. Morgan noticed she smelled faintly of alcohol.

"Um, hi..." Morgan began, timid at first, then broke into her trademark fake smile. "Hi," she repeated, this time with confidence. "You must be Dani's mom."

The woman nodded and narrowed her eyes at Morgan as if trying to recall if they had ever met before.

"I am...and, I'm sorry, have we met?"

"I don't think so, Mrs—Ms.—er...Dr. Rider—"

"Rebecca is fine."

"Rebecca." Morgan smiled again. "I'm Morgan Firestone and this is Isobel Gowdie. We're good friends with Dani from school. In fact, I've picked her up here before—a few weeks ago, actually, but you and I didn't meet face-to-face."

"Oh right...the double date," Rebecca nodded slowly. "Well, what can I do for you girls?"

"We're looking for Dani," Isobel replied casually, smiling broadly. "Just wondered if she was feeling okay."

"Feeling okay?" Rebecca asked, confused. "As far as I know...she was fine this morning before school."

"Oh, so she was at school today?" Morgan asked.

Rebecca stared blankly into space for a beat before she closed her eyes, sighing.

"Girls, is there something I should know?"

"Oh no, no!" Morgan laughed. "No...see, Isobel and I had to retake a test at lunch and we missed her...someone—"

"Another friend of ours, Emma," Isobel added, padding the lie to make it more believable.

"Right, Emma mentioned that Dani wasn't feeling so well at lunch. We don't have any afternoon classes with her and we missed her after school so we thought we would drop by..."

"You know, to check on her," Isobel finished.

Rebecca nodded slowly.

"Well, she's not home yet, but I'm sure she will appreciate your checking in on her." Rebecca glanced over her shoulder into the dark house. "But listen, girls, I have a lot of papers to get back to, so if you don't mind..." she trailed off.

"Of course," Morgan assured her. "We'll leave you to your work. When Dani gets home just tell her we dropped by."

"I will," Rebecca said, shutting the door.

Morgan and Isobel headed back to the car.

"That was weird," Isobel said as soon as both car doors were shut.

"Yeah. Plus, Dani would definitely be home by now if she'd actually gone to school."

"Do you think she knows something?" Isobel asked.

"No," Morgan replied. "She's too wrapped up in her own personal shit to notice."

"Fucking parents," Isobel scoffed. "Speaking of, don't you have therapy this afternoon?"

Morgan glanced at the clock.

"Shit," she whispered. "Yeah—yeah I skipped last week, so I have to go or I'll never hear the end of it."

"Drop me off at the mall?" Isobel asked. "It's on the way."

"Okay, fine. We'll meet up after my session. Keep looking for Dani."

"How much time do we have?"

"I have no idea. It may be too late," Morgan sighed. "If not, I mean, I guess we have until tonight?"

"What happens if we can't...I mean, if we don't..." Isobel trailed off.

Morgan started the car, backing out of Dani's driveway. As she pulled away she thought she saw a face at the upstairs window, but the image had vanished so quickly she couldn't be sure it wasn't just her imagination—though the curtain was still swaying.

"This place gives me the fucking creeps," Isobel said, reaching for another cigarette. Morgan wondered if she'd seen the face as well, but Isobel seemed distracted by her lighter.

"Yeah, same here."

VI

MORGAN WAS SLOUCHED IN the burgundy leather chairs at the Golem Creek Center for Cognitive Behavioral Therapy flipping through a copy of *Yoga Journal* magazine when the receptionist with the frizzy brown hair called her name.

"Morgan?"

Morgan glanced up and lazily dropped the magazine back on the coffee table in front of her. She attempted to smile at the receptionist, but her ability to fake enthusiasm was waning and it came out more like a grimace. It had been a long day. Plus, therapy was bullshit.

"She's ready for you," the receptionist added.

"Thanks," Morgan mumbled as she walked past. Down the hallway, three doors on the left. She knew the drill.

The office smelled like lavender. It was supposed to be calming, but Morgan found it profoundly annoying. The candles, low light, sounds of trickling water from the little fountain in the corner. Morgan disliked this room on a good day; today, she despised it.

The therapist was seated in an easy chair across from the overstuffed couch. Morgan didn't acknowledge her at first. Tossing her purse on the ground, she slumped on the couch and crossed her arms before finally making eye contact.

"Good afternoon, Morgan," the therapist said

warmly.

What a fucking fake, Morgan thought.

"Is it?" she asked.

The therapist scribbled something on her notepad.

"Have you had a stressful day today? What's been going on since we last spoke, uh..." the therapist checked her notes. "Two weeks ago?"

Morgan narrowed her eyes, irritated.

"You knew it was two weeks ago. Don't pretend."

"Well," the therapist began, undeterred. "What's been going on?"

"Nothing," Morgan replied with a sigh. "Nothing at all. Trying to keep shit together...girls at school don't know what's best for them, everything falls to me as usual. That's all."

"And you feel it's your job to...step in?"

"Yes."

"And why do you feel this way? Why would that fall to you?"

Morgan rolled her eyes and sighed, examining her fingernails.

"With great power comes great responsibility."

"I'm afraid I don't understand. What power?"

"What's that from, anyway?" Morgan asked, wishing there was a window in this goddamn room so she could have something, anything, to look at besides inspirational posters of marathon runners and the beach.

"Your feelings of power and responsibility?"

"No," Morgan rolled her eyes. "The quote."

"Oh," the therapist frowned. "I think...Voltaire."

"Are you sure?" Morgan thought a moment. "Because I'm pretty sure it's Spider-Man."

"Well, it doesn't really matter, now does it?" the therapist asked. "What matters is that these are your feelings—that you feel you've been given some sort of power over your peers, and with that power comes the weight of responsibility. I'm simply asking—"

"You don't like that answer?" Morgan asked, happy to belabor the point. "It's a good quote. You really want it to be Voltaire, don't you?"

"Well, I'm not here to 'like' anything you say, Morgan. You know that. I'm simply hoping that you could clarify why you feel you have this responsibility to—"

"Here's a better answer for you," Morgan said sharply, suddenly bored by the whole situation and ready to cut to the chase. "Maybe you'll like this one: I have a pathological need to fix everything for everyone to make up for the fact that I have no control at home—"

"Morgan," the therapist interjected.

"No, no...I think this is good. Get all this out in the open. Yeah, I have an absent father—a criminal, no less—and an absent mother who could be around more often if she wasn't...oh! If she wasn't too busy with her own pathological need to fix fucking everything for fucking everyone."

"Morgan—"

"Seriously, mom, these sessions are a joke."

"Morgan," her mother repeated. "This doesn't work if you break the wall like that. If you feel the need to vent to your therapist about your mother and her—how did you put it?" She glanced down at her notes again. "Her 'pathological need to fix fucking everything for fucking everyone,' then you should be completely free to do so. I'm here in my professional capacity as your therapist, not as your mother."

"Well, naturally. That *is* your primary role, isn't it?"

"As your therapist, I fully understand your resentment toward your mother. And you should feel completely free to continue to explore those feelings..." She paused to clear her throat. "However, I should remind you that these sessions are intended to explore your feelings about your *father*, following his incarceration. So perhaps I can steer your thoughts in that direction for the remainder of our session?"

Morgan rolled her eyes. This was complete bullshit. She had other things to do—find Dani, save Dani from going down the same path she and Isobel went down four years ago, figure out what Giles meant about growing powers... She couldn't waste any more time on her mother's bizarre pseudo-therapeutic ego trip.

It was then that Morgan decided to give these growing powers a try on someone besides her friends. Her mother, as usual, was busy scribbling notes on her legal pad, obviously avoiding eye contact.

"Mom," she said flatly.

Her mother didn't look up.

"*Mom*," she repeated, a bit more insistently.

Nothing.

Realizing that in order to best her mother she would first have to start out by playing her inane game, she cleared her throat.

"Dr. Firestone?"

"Mmmhmm?" Morgan's mother replied, still

scribbling away. It wasn't eye contact, but it was something.

"I'm not doing this anymore," Morgan stated. "Dad is in jail with all the other white-collar criminals—well, all the other criminals. You can't do anything about that, so you're trying to fix me. Either that or you're using me as an excuse to talk through your feelings about him. Just like he used to use me for his scams. You're both bad people. I'm out."

Morgan realized halfway through her speech that she didn't need powers this time. Telling her mother the truth was enough to shock her into submission.

Morgan's mother, her pen frozen on the yellow legal pad, finally raised her eyes to meet her daughter's gaze, but Morgan was halfway out the door.

"Morgan—" she called, almost absentmindedly.

"What?" Morgan snapped, turning back toward the office. "Let me guess: you won't be home until late? What a shock."

Morgan started to slam the office door behind her, but realized it wasn't worth it. She rushed out of the building just as she felt tears welling up in her eyes. She knew exactly who she needed to call to start to unravel this mess, but he was the last person on the planet she wanted to talk to.

Once in her car, Morgan checked her makeup in her visor mirror once again, this time to make sure her tears hadn't caused her mascara to run. Satisfied by her reflection, she reached into her glove compartment where Isobel had been digging around earlier and pulled out the emergency cigarettes and lighter.

"Time to make some bad decisions," she muttered

to herself, lighting a cigarette and taking a long inhale. Her confidence bolstered by a few more drags, Morgan fished in her purse for her phone and hit "1" on her speed dial. He answered, of course.

"Hey, asshole. Wanna come over?"

VII

THE FIRST TIME MORGAN and Giles hooked up it was a few days after that first night at The Spot. She wasn't even sure why she called him. "Trauma bonding," or some shit her mother might say. At the time, he was the only person who knew what she'd been through in the woods that night. Morgan didn't care to think about it too much. He was attractive and willing, so she kept it up. Morgan wasn't sure if Isobel had been doing the same thing, but she had her suspicions. Still, it didn't really matter in the long run—and it certainly didn't matter today. Today all that mattered was that Giles tell her what was going to happen with Dani.

Giles was laying on her bed smoking a cigarette. Morgan was sitting in front of her vanity brushing her hair.

"So come on—tell me the truth about tonight," Morgan addressed Giles from the mirror. He sat up and met her eyes in the reflection.

"What are you talking about?"

"What's going on with Dani? What were you talking about earlier?"

"When?"

"Fuck you, Giles. *You* know. When Isobel and I ran into you waiting on Zach."

Giles exhaled, obviously irritated.

"What do you see in Zach, anyway?" he asked,

avoiding the question.

Morgan decided to play along.

"He's human, for one thing."

"Boring."

"He's my age—hey, speaking of, how old *are* you, anyway? I can't believe I've never asked you that."

"Old as time, my dear."

Morgan rolled her eyes and continued.

"He protects me from *you*."

"Need I remind you that you're the one who always calls me for these...assignations."

"He doesn't use words like 'assignations.'"

"That's certainly true."

"I don't know. He makes me look good at school. What can I say?"

Giles grinned, satisfied.

"Your vanity knows no bounds, Morgan. It's one of the things I've always liked best about you. A lovely quality."

Morgan put down her hairbrush, turned from the mirror, and wandered back over to the bed, sitting down next to Giles and taking his cigarette.

"Yeah, well, enough about me," she said, taking a drag. She'd been smoking a lot today. Bad day, bad habits.

"You know," Giles said, taking back the cigarette, "you never ask about me—*my* day, *my* hopes and dreams. How do you suppose that makes me feel?"

"You're a demon. I assume you don't have any hopes or dreams." Morgan paused. "Or feelings, for that matter."

"That's an unfair assumption."

"Come on, Giles."

"And an incorrect one, actually," Giles continued, suddenly thoughtful. "If you knew anything about so-called mythical creatures—which, given your circumstances, you probably should—"

"I called you for a reason—"

"And I'm pretty sure that reason has been...satisfied," Giles smirked.

"You know what I mean," Morgan snapped.

"You know—I have to say, Morgan, you act all high and mighty because, as you so bluntly point out, I'm a demon—an assumption, by the way, but let's assume it's true. Unless I'm mistaken, *you're* the one who called on a 'demon,' and who has continued to call on a 'demon' repeatedly for what...four years now? So maybe what you should be asking yourself is what that says about *you*."

Morgan didn't want to think about that.

"Tell me what you know. Tell me your plan—his plan, whatever."

"Morgan, I don't know what more you want from me. I've told you everything—multiple times, in fact. You made a deal with him. You got what you wanted, and you're about to get more. But part of all this, the power that you had in high school and the power that you're gaining now, was always dependent on his getting a third. And you've managed to intimidate away all other potential offerings—"

"That's what you call them? 'Offerings'? That's great, Giles."

"What can I say? I'm a poet," he laughed.

"Was that all I was to you? An offering to him?"

Giles's eyes grew dark and his tone suddenly serious.

"No. You were—are...different."

Morgan glared at him and stormed back over to her vanity, sitting down with her back to him.

"I'm sure you say that to all the girls."

"You've scared them all away," Giles continued. "I know you two think you beat the system, and I hate to be the one to tell you this—"

"No you don't."

"Okay, fine. I love it. I love to be the one to tell you this: you can't beat the devil. You signed up for this, Morgan. You can't protect Dani. It's already happened."

Morgan turned around furiously and threw her hairbrush at Giles. He ducked, laughing.

"What do you mean it's already happened?" she demanded. "You're saying you took her out there yesterday?"

"I'm taking her out there right now," Giles laughed. "Don't you know? I really thought you knew."

"Knew what?" Morgan snapped.

"You're asleep, Morgan," he said gently, cupping her face in his hands. "And when you wake up it will be too late."

VIII

AT THAT MOMENT, MORGAN'S room melted around her. The pink and gold of her bedroom swirled together before her eyes, distorting her vision. Giles vanished, but Morgan still felt his cold gaze upon her as she came to. She was at The Spot. At least, she *thought* it was The Spot. It was dark, and she was alone in the middle of the forest. She could see the full moon through the trees. She felt oddly disconnected from her body, but she pulled herself up off the damp leaves and leaned against a tree.

That's when she heard the chanting.

It seemed to emanate from somewhere beneath her. She looked down at the earth below her feet and noticed that it was shaking. She bent down, kneeling on her knees, and pressed her ear to the ground. The chanting was coming from somewhere deep below the surface. Frantic, she started digging, her fingernails cutting through the leaves and dirt until the ground opened up before her and she could see an orange light emanating from somewhere at the other end of the hole. The chanting grew louder and, before she knew what she was doing, she plunged through.

IX

THAT HAD A BEEN a week ago.

The morning after the dream Morgan woke up in a cold sweat. Dirt under her fingernails, but everything else pretty much in order. A deep sense of unease, but nothing particularly out of the ordinary.

After the dream, she pretended nothing had happened. It wasn't that hard to do, really. She could barely remember a thing—either from the dream, or from the day before. She vaguely recalled that she and Isobel had been upset about something regarding Dani, but she couldn't remember exactly what. She felt vaguely unnerved by the dream, but she couldn't quite remember why. She confided in Zach, and he helped comfort her. Stayed on the phone with her until she fell asleep. Nice things like that. He really was a good boyfriend—so simple, so understanding. She avoided Giles. Went out of her way to avoid him. *He* really was an *asshole*—even if she couldn't quite remember why. She made plans for homecoming, she got her nails done. Everything was just fine. Pleasant, even.

Until, that is, it all came rushing back.

It was Saturday, the morning of the homecoming dance, exactly one week after Morgan woke up amnesiac and spent a week of blissful ignorance.

Lazily flipping through her English textbook, she paused, transfixed by a William Blake painting. There was something familiar about the image that she couldn't place at first. Suddenly she was gripped with a splitting headache—and that's when it happened. Unable to stay restrained any longer, the memories came rushing back to her. Piles of bodies like animated clay writhing in the mud. Hoards of women chanting around the roaring fire. And Morgan joining in—readily, easily. Isobel was there, and Dani too. But it wasn't just the three of them. A mass of women, wild-eyed women, dancing and chanting around the bonfire. Morgan thought she recognized more in the mass than just Isobel and Dani, but she wasn't sure. Even as the memories flooded over her she felt confused by them, as if she had been both present and absent at the same time. She certainly couldn't place the location. It was as if they were underground but on top of the earth at the same time—the heels of her feet digging into the mud, deeper than the tree roots, her hair tangling around the stars.

And then a familiar figure—the creature she'd come to know so well from their meetings at The Spot—presiding silently over the group, gazing down at the mud-caked mass of bodies, wings spread like a vulture.

Morgan covered her eyes with her hands, trying and failing to physically block out the memories. But they continued to assault her. She remembered everything—the day before, the rumors about Dani and Giles, meeting Isobel at The Spot during fourth period, Dani's house, the therapy session, Giles.

"Giles—fucking Giles," she muttered, dropping her hands from her eyes and suddenly enraged.

She reached for her phone, but paused, unsure

of who she wanted to call. Giles owed her an explanation, but she didn't trust him. Especially not after what he'd just pulled. It was Isobel she needed to talk to, but she felt nervous. At that moment, Morgan's phone rang. Morgan answered.

"Fucking Giles," Isobel spat.

Morgan felt her entire body relax. Isobel knew. At least they could be honest with each other, maybe try to piece some of this mess together.

"When did you remember?" Morgan asked, relieved.

"Just a few minutes ago. What a fucking asshole. He totally lied to us in the woods. He's been lying to us since day one. And now..." Isobel trailed off.

"What?" Morgan asked. "Now what?"

"I don't know." Morgan could hear Isobel smoking on the other end of the line. "Meet me somewhere? I don't know if I want to talk about it over the phone."

Morgan felt her stomach clench with anxiety. She knew where they needed to meet, but it was the last place on earth she wanted to go.

"The Spot?" she ventured wearily.

"That fucking place," Isobel sighed.

"We don't have a lot of options," Morgan replied.

"I know."

"We can't exactly talk about this stuff anywhere."

"I know."

"I mean, if you really don't want..." Morgan trailed off, knowing full well that The Spot was the only place she and Isobel could speak freely.

"No, no," she could hear Isobel grabbing her purse and keys, heading out the door. "It's the only place. See you in twenty?"

"Yeah," Morgan agreed. "See you soon."

"Hey," Isobel interjected suddenly. "Call Dani. She's in this shit now too, I guess."

X

FIFTEEN MINUTES LATER, MORGAN stood at the edge of the woods, knowing full well that if she walked in nothing would be the same again. Morgan wasn't sure exactly what would change—she'd already had the dream (if it had even been a dream—she still wasn't completely sure). She and Isobel and Dani were somehow connected by the very magic she'd willed into her life four years ago. But there was something about this day, something about the action of acknowledging everything upfront, that made her feel deeply uneasy.

Morgan hadn't called Dani—hadn't picked up the phone, that is. She was trying something out. Giles had said her powers were growing.

She decided to test them. Closing her eyes, she'd pictured Dani perfectly in her mind, whispered her name, summoned her to The Spot, and seen Dani nod in reply.

Morgan glanced at her watch. Isobel would be there already. It was time to move.

"Now or never," she muttered, partly to herself, partly to the trees, and stepped over the threshold of the forest onto crinkled fall leaves.

As Morgan walked through the woods, a trail she'd traversed countless times over the past four years, she felt overwhelmed by a sense of growing awareness she'd never felt before. The trees seemed to bend and contort for her as she walked; she saw faces in the twisted roots, heard the rustling of an animal somehow just behind and just in front of her. She had the overarching sense that she was not alone—a sense that was both unsettling and somehow comforting all at once.

When she reached The Spot, Isobel was waiting, slouched against a tree.

"Hey," Morgan called out as she approached.

"What the fuck?" Isobel demanded.

"I don't know."

"What happened?"

"I don't know."

"You were supposed to pick me up at the mall after your therapy session—"

"I know. I'm sorry." Morgan paused, unsure if she wanted to admit to Isobel that she'd called Giles. She decided to wait. "How did you get home?"

"I ran into Giles outside the mall and he gave me a ride," Isobel replied, rolling her eyes.

"Giles?" Morgan asked.

"Yeah," Isobel continued. "He asked if I was still mad at him. I said I didn't give a fuck, and could he give me a ride home. And the next thing I know I'm waking up in my bed, everything's cool... I mean, I'd forgotten everything from the previous day, but whatever. Everything seemed fine. Until it all came rushing back just this afternoon."

Morgan sat down on a fallen branch, her thoughts reeling.

"You ran into Giles?"

"Yeah," Isobel had started to pace.

"What time?"

"I don't know, maybe an hour and a half after you

dropped me off. Why?"

"That's impossible," Morgan said, shaking her head.

"Why?"

"He was with *me*. He was at my house."

Isobel stopped pacing and glared at Morgan.

"We're in this together, so I'm not going to be mad at you because, frankly, we're all we have right now. But thanks a lot for ditching me—that sucks, Morgan."

"I didn't mean to," Morgan groaned, putting her head in her hands. "I was upset. I asked him to come over for a quickie...I figured I'd pick you up right afterwards."

Isobel sat down next to Morgan.

"It's okay," Isobel said, putting her arm around Morgan's shoulders. "It was a weird fucking day."

"No kidding."

"And then you just woke up the next morning?"

"Yeah."

"You think he did something to us?" Isobel asked.

"Like what?"

"Drugged us? A spell? I don't know. Something."

"I don't know... Weirdly, I don't think so," Morgan ventured. "It feels more complicated than that. Besides—"

Morgan stopped short at the sound of leaves crunching underfoot. Someone was approaching.

Morgan and Isobel stood up just as Dani stepped into the circle.

"You called for me?" Dani said, looking right at Morgan, who burst out laughing.

"Holy shit...yeah, yeah I did."

XI

Morgan, Isobel, and Dani were seated in silence on logs around the remains of a campfire in the center of The Spot.

Dani was the first to break the silence.

"I'm sorry—you did *what*?" she demanded.

"We made a deal," Morgan stated simply.

"You made a deal with the devil...for popularity?"

"First of all," Isobel began. "Popularity is a very simplistic way of—"

"It wasn't just about being popular," Morgan broke in.

"Also, we don't know he's the devil. We don't actually know what he is. A lesser demon or something, I don't know," Isobel continued.

"You really think that matters? A 'lesser demon' is so much better than the devil?"

"It might be," Isobel said. "The thing is, we don't know."

"And you signed his book, and you...did things..." Dani didn't finish her sentence, she just shook her head.

"It's complicated," Morgan said flatly. "We were young, we wanted something...and, to restate the point: it wasn't just popularity, okay."

"And, I mean, we never meant for it to get this..." Isobel started.

"Out of hand," Morgan finished for her.

Dani was staring off into space, her eyes round,

unblinking.

"And Giles..." Dani trailed off.

"Oh, Giles is definitely...*something*. Involved," Morgan answered. "That we know for sure."

"Fucking Giles," Isobel muttered.

"He's more like an errand boy."

"More like a fuck boy," Isobel added.

"Well...he serves a few purposes," Morgan added.

Dani shook her head in disbelief.

"This is so...this is seriously messed up."

"It is what it is," Isobel shrugged. "We made the choice."

"So you're what? Witches?"

Morgan glanced at Isobel. They'd never actually used that term, but it felt right.

"I mean, I guess so."

"And you just use your power for what...a bunch of meaningless, vapid bullshit? You were given the opportunity to ask for all the power in the world... anything you wanted, to do whatever you wanted with. And you chose, what? Chanel bags and perfect hair and getting voted Prom Queen every year?"

Isobel rolled her eyes.

"Partly," Morgan began. "But also to protect the girls at Honorius. To keep them away from Giles, keep them out of the woods at night, keep them from making the same mistake that we made."

"You know, we do a lot for the girls at this school," Isobel added, narrowing her eyes at Dani. "You should be grateful. Or, at least, you *would* be grateful if you'd fallen in line like the rest of them."

"Excuse me?" Dani demanded. "You're blaming me for this?"

"You're the one who kissed Giles on the senior trip," Isobel continued. "And you know what else? You're standing there judging us, but you fell for all this too. You didn't get dragged into this against your will. The only way this works is if you wanted something too. You're not so innocent, Danielle. What did you ask for? What bargain did you make?"

"I didn't make one," Dani replied.

"Bullshit," Isobel snapped.

"No. You know what? *You're* bullshit. Pretending like you're doing girls at this school a favor—by what? Keeping them in line? Being a bully? That's not helping anyone but yourselves and your massive egos."

"Don't change the subject," Isobel warned her. "If you were there—here, whatever—that night it means you must have signed the book too. So stop acting so offended. What was it? What was it that you asked for?"

"I didn't. I didn't ask for anything. I didn't do anything. Giles kissed me on that trip—ask anyone."

"Yeah, right," Isobel laughed.

Morgan had been sitting back silently watching Dani during this interaction, listening—not to her words, but to something else, something deep inside Dani she wasn't even sure Dani could hear herself.

"You're lying," Morgan said, locking eyes with Dani.

Dani shifted under Morgan's gaze.

"No I'm not."

"Oh, you absolutely are." Morgan paused, narrowing her eyes and attempting to tune back into the current. It was rushing. "I can hear it. And I can either figure it out myself, or I can *make* you tell us."

"What are you talking about?" Dani asked warily.

"Just like how I made you come here today. You heard me in your head, didn't you? I saw you when I called. I can make you do whatever I want, and you know it. And I want you to tell us the truth. Right now."

At that moment, Dani glanced at one of the other logs surrounding the fire pit and, with a quick jerk of her head, sent the log flying at Morgan.

Morgan ducked, avoiding the log.

"What the fuck?" Isobel cried, jumping up and backing away from the circle.

Morgan, somewhat shaken, stood up too.

Dani had already taken off through the woods.

"It's fine," Morgan said calmly. "I know how to find her."

XII

Isobel and Morgan sat in silence for some time.

Isobel reached into her purse and pulled out a flask, offering Morgan the first swig.

Morgan took a long drink.

"Are we ever going to talk about this?" she asked, handing the flask back to Isobel. Isobel sighed.

"What specifically do you want to talk about? Haven't we covered everything?"

"The beginning, I mean...we never really talked about..."

"What we asked for?"

"Yeah. How it happened. How all this started."

Isobel took a drink and handed the flask back to Morgan.

"Did you really ask for popularity? Was that it?"

"No," Morgan muttered. "I just wanted to be seen. I wanted power. I wanted people to listen to me for once. It sounds stupid now, but at the time..." she trailed off.

"Yeah," Isobel nodded. "Power."

"I don't think we're supposed to want that."

"Nope," Isobel said, closing her eyes and taking another swig.

"At least not admit it."

"Right."

"What about you?"

"Same," Isobel began. "I wanted power. I wanted to be prepared—to be ready for shit. I was so sick of the goddamn rug being pulled out from under me."

"Your dad?"

"Yeah," Isobel whispered. "Screw him," she finished quietly.

"Screw him," Morgan added, reaching out for Isobel's hand.

The girls sat there a moment longer before Isobel stood up and began pacing.

"So when did you meet Giles, anyway?"

Morgan thought back. He'd been such a big part of her life for so long it was hard to remember. "The summer before ninth grade definitely. Maybe June? Late June."

"Same here. June 24th," Isobel said.

"You remember the date?" Morgan asked. "That sounds right, actually. June 24th. That's a weird day for me anyway."

"Yeah," Isobel continued, taking another drink and handing Morgan the flask. "My dad's birthday."

Morgan felt a shock resonate throughout her body.

"Wait, what?"

"What?" Isobel replied, continuing to pace.

"You never told me your dad's birthday was June 24th."

"Does it matter?"

"Well it's weird...I mean, that's my dad's birthday too."

"Seriously?"

Both girls sat back down in front of the fire pit.

"Yeah," Morgan said. "That's weird, right?"

"That's super weird."

"And Giles, you...I mean how did you know how

to find him? Or did—"

"I didn't, he found me."

"Same here."

"I don't know why I assumed…" Isobel trailed off.

"I did too," Morgan added. "But I was wandering through the woods. That's right, it was the 24th. My mom is always a nutcase on that day… I just needed to get out of the house. And he just appeared from behind a tree. I thought he was…"

"So cute," Isobel laughed.

"Yep," Morgan laughed too. "And, I don't know, we started talking. I didn't realize the extent of…I didn't really understand what I was getting into." She paused for another drink. "And then later that night…I mean, you know the drill. The book, the ritual, all that."

"Yeah," Isobel whispered. "Fucking scary shit."

"So fucking scary."

"I thought I was dead," Isobel continued. Morgan noticed that her hands were shaking. "Like, seriously. Thought I'd died and that…that was that. That I was dead and in hell and it was all over. It was the worst feeling I can…" She trailed off for a moment before pulling herself back together. "And then I woke up the next morning and everything seemed different. I mean, not just different. The world seemed like an easier place. I felt stronger, you know? Like a better version of myself."

"Yeah, totally."

"I can't believe we've never talked about this before. It was like, serious fucking trauma. PTSD shit."

"We didn't have to talk about it. We just…we were

just there for each other. That's what was important then—now, too. It's okay," Morgan said, suddenly exhausted by the whole situation, rubbing her eyes with the heels of her hands. "All that mattered was that we knew, and we had each other, and we trusted each other, and we were going to keep anyone else from having to take that on."

Isobel stood and started to pace again.

"Do you think it's true—what Dani said?"

"What about this just being about our egos?"

"Yeah."

"Probably," Morgan sighed. "I was such a bitch to her."

"Well she was lying to us."

"Right...right."

"She got herself into this mess as much as we did," Isobel continued.

"But that's the thing," Morgan interjected. "That's the thing. I mean, did we? All this time I've been blaming myself—but if Giles found us...and found us both on that day—that day that weirdly connects us. I mean, what does that say? Was he looking for us?"

"I mean, yeah. It had to be," Isobel added.

"Yeah. So why us? Why that night?"

"And why Dani, now?"

"You know who we have to talk to," Morgan said wearily.

"Don't remind me," Isobel groaned.

"He's the only one who might be able to...he's our only chance at figuring any of this shit out. He started it, after all."

"Do you even know where to find him?" Isobel asked.

Morgan paused. She suddenly realized that in all the years she'd known Giles she never once asked where he lived. The realization that she actually knew nothing about him slowly washed over her.

"I guess I don't...but *you* might," Morgan began.

"What do you mean?"

"Your visions, you know. I mean, why not give it a try? See if you can...I don't know, locate him or whatever."

Isobel sat down on a fallen tree trunk and closed her eyes. Within only a few seconds her eyes opened, dilated, flashing lavender.

"The abandoned storage shed at the other end of the forest," she said as her eyes slowly shifted back to blue-grey.

"The one by the cemetery?"

"Yeah."

"Seriously?" Morgan asked, impressed but wary.

"I actually don't know...it was fuzzy, like an old black and white picture. I didn't see Giles, but I definitely recognized that shed."

"How do you feel?" Morgan asked.

Isobel shook her head and shivered.

"Weird."

"It didn't make you sick or anything?"

"No," Isobel said, rubbing her eyes. "Just weird. I don't know how to explain it. It's fine, though. I'm fine. You should go, go check it out...see if you can get something—anything out of him. Try, at least."

"Okay," Morgan said, unsure if she should leave her friend.

"He'll never give us a straight answer."

"Maybe," Morgan ventured. "Maybe. But he

was being honest about one thing. Our powers are growing. I don't know if they'll work on him, but it's worth a shot. And if I can't make him talk, maybe just being around him will trigger something in you."

"Another vision, you mean?"

"Yeah. It's worth a try, right? As long as you're okay..." Morgan trailed off.

"I'm fine now, really," Isobel reassured her. "It was like I was totally drained there for a minute, but it's better now."

"I guess we're both still learning," Morgan sighed. "We'll figure it out."

"What about Dani?" Isobel asked.

"It would be useful if we could have her there too, right? I mean, who knows what else she's capable of?"

"She was pretty pissed."

Morgan sighed. "I probably deserved it," she said. "Remember, we've had four years to come to terms with this shit. She's had, what...?"

"A day?" Isobel shook her head. "That's a lot to take in."

"Yeah. So, okay. We'll let her hide a little while longer," Morgan shrugged. "She'll be easy to find. If I can't summon her, I'm sure you can find her... psychically, or whatever. We'll give her a little time to cool off. She's scared. I don't think she's going to be much trouble."

"That was pretty badass when she threw that log with her mind," Isobel laughed.

"Absolutely," Morgan agreed. "We'll figure this shit out. And we'll all come out on top. Like we always do."

XIII

THE CLOSER MORGAN GOT to the shed at the other side of the woods the angrier she became. By the time she could see the dilapidated building in the distance she was positively enraged. Her life before Giles had been perfectly fine. All this was his fault—he had preyed on her desires, preyed on all the things that he somehow knew occupied her dreams. Maybe she was partly to blame for what happened—but what other fourteen-year-old girl doesn't want the very things she had asked for? Power, popularity, control. She had spent years with a sour feeling in the pit of her stomach, outwardly pleased with the shape her life had taken, but inwardly beating herself up for the desires that she considered so...

"So *what*?" she demanded, stomping over the brittle red leaves, the cemetery gates now fully in sight.

So embarrassing, taboo, unfeminine. Things nice girls weren't supposed to want. Things nice girls weren't supposed to even think about. Sexual desire, desire for authority, desire to be listened to, desire for influence, power. Nice girls aren't supposed to desire—period.

"*Bullshit*," she muttered, grinding her teeth and picking up her pace.

If it hadn't been for Giles—if it hadn't been for the fact that wanting those things required a deal with the devil...

She paused to take a deep breath when she realized she'd arrived at the shed.

"Giles!" she cried.

No answer.

"Giles!" she repeated. "Get out here, you motherfucker. You have a *hell* of a lot of explaining to do."

Nothing.

Morgan took another deep breath. Maybe Isobel had been wrong. Neither of them were quite sure how these powers worked yet.

Just when Morgan was about to give up and turn back around, the scent of cigarette smoke hit her nostrils. It was coming from inside the shed.

"Fucking asshole," she mumbled as she moved toward the shed. "You don't want to come out, I'm coming in."

Morgan threw open the door and stifled a gasp.

XIV

"WHAT THE..." MORGAN BEGAN.

"Morgan," Giles said, taking a drag on his cigarette, not looking up. A statement of fact rather than a greeting.

"I—" Morgan started, but faltered, turning away to face the other direction.

"It's fine, Morgan. You can look."

"I'm not sure I...want to," Morgan said, still turned away.

"As you wish," she heard Giles mutter.

Morgan took a deep breath and turned back around. There, slumped on the floor of the abandoned shed, was a half-goat, half-man somewhat resembling Giles but heavily bearded and with giant curling horns jutting out from the sides of his head.

"So..." Morgan couldn't finish her thought.

"It's time you knew, I guess," Giles sighed, flicking his cigarette into a corner of the room. Morgan, unsure of what else to do, marched over and stomped on it.

"Knew what, exactly?"

"My true form," Giles replied, sighing again, heavier this time as if he was already exhausted by the conversation.

"So you're a...what? What *is* this?"

"I'm a satyr," Giles said, crossing his hairy arms across his chest.

"Okay...and what's a satyr?"

"A nature spirit. Come on, surely you've heard of us...Bacchus? Pan?" Morgan shook her head. "Fun fact," Giles continued. "Socrates was one of us...not a lot of people know that. Nathaniel Hawthorne—"

"Like *The Scarlet Letter*? From English class? He was—"

"No, no," Giles shook his black curls, laughing. "No, but he wrote *The Marble Faun*."

"Faun?"

"It's basically the same thing," Giles added casually before continuing. "Malarmé and Debussy made us quite famous in the nineteenth century."

"Who?" Morgan asked, starting to feel irritated.

"Stephane Malarmé and Claude Debussy... *L'après-midi d'un faune*, you know..."

"I don't know."

"Nijinsky—" Giles began.

"Stop showing off, Giles," Morgan interrupted, rolling her eyes.

"Showing off?!" Giles demanded, incredulous. "Look at me, Morgan. I don't have a lot of dignity here. I'm just trying to—oh! Mr. Tumnus?"

"Oh right..." Morgan said slowly. "I see. So... you're...from...Narnia?"

Giles groaned and lit another cigarette.

"*The Chronicles of Narnia* is a book series, Morgan. By C.S. Lewis. This," he motioned to their surroundings. "This...piece of shit world is reality."

"Don't talk to me like I'm stupid," Morgan spat. "You just told me you're a fucking faun—or satyr, or whatever. I didn't know those were real. Who knows! Maybe Narnia is real too—all fucking bets are off now, apparently."

"I apologize," Giles conceded, closing his eyes and blowing two tendrils of smoke out his nostrils.

"So are you the only one...or...?"

"In this area, yes. I've been the only one for some time. I suppose there are probably others like me around the globe...but I don't know," Giles opened his eyes and stared blankly into space. "I have no way of knowing, and I haven't for some time."

"Were you born here?" Morgan asked.

"No...I was brought here a very, very long time ago."

"By who?"

"Whom," Giles corrected.

"Oh my god," Morgan rolled her eyes.

"I'd really rather not talk about it," Giles sighed.

"Well I've got news for you, asshole. You've got a lot to talk about. And I'm not leaving until you do. And, thanks to you, I guess, I now possess the powers to make you talk. So we can do this the easy way, or the hard way. It's up to you."

Giles stared at Morgan for what seemed like an incredibly long time. Morgan felt her heart beat faster, but she was determined to not let her anxiety show. Besides, there was something in his eyes that made her deeply sad, rather than angry.

"I suppose this is a long time coming," Giles said.

"No kidding," Morgan replied.

Giles took one more drag on his cigarette.

"The year was 1922..."

XV

Now it was Morgan's turn to be incredulous.

"*Excuse me?*" she demanded.

"Come on, Morgan," Giles sighed. "You knew I was older..."

"Yeah, old*er*. Not old."

"Do you want to hear the story or not?" Giles asked, tossing his cigarette onto the cracked wood floor of the shed.

Morgan crossed her arms over her chest and sighed.

"Continue, please."

"It was 1922. Prohibition. Everyone knows about your standard speakeasys, but what a lot of people don't know is the role that magic played in a number of these...underground soirées."

Giles lit another cigarette and took a long drag.

"At the turn of the century I was happily employed in both Paris and London. Going back and forth across the pond whenever a particularly intriguing event called to me. Worked the party circuit with the notable aesthetes and decadents of the day. For a satyr, the fin-de-siècle was the time to be alive. The absolute highlight of my career—"

"*Career?*" Morgan asked, arching an eyebrow.

"Yes, Morgan," Giles snapped. "Career. To put it in your terms, satyrs at the fin-de-siècle were like... socialites, celebrities. In the twentieth century we evolved into icons. Holly Golightly, or the Club Kids in the '90s, or…" he trailed off, sighing. "Paris Hilton, to dumb it down a bit, I suppose. But you get the point. We weren't freaks, or monsters, or relics of the past. We made your party the place to be. We *were* the party. And we were in massive demand at the turn of the century. I went from wild nights in Paris drinking flaming absinthe on tabletops with Arthur Rimbaud and Charles Baudelaire, to setting ornate peacock-feathered tablescapes for Oscar Wilde and Aubrey Beardsley in London." Giles paused and stared into space for a moment before continuing. "And these were more than just parties, Morgan. We had influence. We were like muses then. Magic was everywhere—you couldn't escape it. Especially in high society and among the artists. The air was tinged with a sense of dread as the century drew to a close, and for some reason that dread led to a flood of creative expression." Giles stopped to finish his cigarette and smash it into the floor. "But all things must come to an end. We had a few more good years, but after Wilde's imprisonment everything started to change, and by the time he died the decadent scene was on the wane in Europe. I even tried to work—actually work, you know, start up something in publishing. A failed arts magazine for the remainder of the decadent set. But interest was low. It seemed like we were to be relegated once again to myth—the annals of forgotten history. However, when Prohibition hit the States, we knew it was time to make our move across the Atlantic."

"So…you just decided to move over here? And what? Start your business up again?" Morgan asked, sliding down into a sitting position against the wall of the shed.

"Not...exactly," Giles replied. "It wasn't that simple, you see. Being a magical creature, I have to take some precautions. There are always those who... well, hunters, to put it simply. Collectors. Those who seek us out, attempt to enslave us. I thought I'd done my research, but..." Giles trailed off.

"But what?" Morgan asked, sitting forward. "You were what? Brought over here as a slave?"

"Not at first," Giles interjected. "I was propositioned by a man named Raymond Clarke. A man of means. A magician. He'd attended one of my parties back in London—a soirée at the residence of the author Arthur Machen. He wrote to me in 1921 and suggested a move overseas to help him get something started in Golem Creek."

"Get something started?"

"A secret society of sorts...a society of magicians. He employed me for these gatherings to enhance the experience. The job was to be somewhat similar to what I'd done in Europe, but without the artistic panache. *Lots* of alcohol. Revelry, and so forth. But, unfortunately, Dr. Clarke was a gambler—and a bad one at that. And he lost me."

"He *lost* you?"

"Yes."

"What the hell is that supposed to mean?"

"It's not supposed to mean anything—you get the idea. He lost me. To...The Creature."

"The Creature? Who is 'The Creature'?"

"You—you've met," Giles said hesitantly.

Morgan felt her stomach turn.

"Okay, so what? So you just stayed with him?"

Morgan demanded. "Doing his bidding? Kidnapping high school girls?"

"He instructed me to seek you out...mollify you, bring you into the fold."

"*Kidnap* us?" Morgan interjected.

"No—offer you something. Whatever it was that you most desired. Make it seem as if this was the only way. Bring you to him—"

"By kidnapping us," Morgan finished for him.

"I repeat, no—"

"Oh my god," Morgan gasped, laughing.

"What?" Giles demanded, annoyed.

"That is such a Tumnus move."

"Excuse me?"

"Mr. Tumnus. From Narnia. He totally kidnaps kids and brings them to the White Witch. That's his entire purpose. At the beginning, I mean. You're *totally* Mr. Tumnus."

"As I said before, Morgan, this isn't...that was a book from 1950..."

"Whatever, dude," Morgan laughed. "All you fauns must be the same."

"I really prefer the term satyr."

"Satyr, whatever."

"Besides, I didn't...you weren't...it's not like you were a sacrifice. You were always going to have this power. You were always a witch. You understand that, right? That was already within you. I didn't do anything—he didn't really do anything..."

"Except convince me that I owed him something."

"Well, yes."

"And it's not like you were completely innocent, either. You kept that charade up until...let's see, just now."

"I understand why you're angry," Giles began. "But what was I supposed to do? He's had me captive for over a century. I don't have a lot of choice in this matter. The only freedom I'm allowed is to spend time with you—"

"Don't flatter me," Morgan snapped.

"I wouldn't dare."

"Besides, you spend time with other people. Isobel, *Dani*... I know you hang out with Zach. We saw you just the other day."

"Isobel and Dani are the same story..." he trailed off. "For the most part."

"And Zach?" Morgan asked, rolling her eyes. "You mean to tell me Zach is a witch too?"

Giles lit another cigarette and gazed down at the ground, inhaling slowly.

"Morgan...there's something you need to know about Zach."

"Oh really?" Morgan asked, turning to leave. "Really? Something about Zach? You know what, coming from someone who basically kidnapped me, sold me to a monster, lied to me for four years, and all the while regularly had sex with me—"

"Purely consensual," Giles interjected. "And always at your behest."

"Not the point," Morgan retorted. "We're done here. You're done—dead to me. I don't give a shit what you have to say about Zach, or anyone else in this fucked up town for that matter."

"I—"

"What could you possibly say? Did Zach make a deal too? At this point I don't care. We all screwed up, and we're all screwed. But at least we have each other. You're just alone in your fucking shed by the goddamn cemetery. And you know what?" Morgan asked, turning furiously towards the door. "I don't care about you," she lied through gritted teeth. "I never cared about you, and I don't care about you now. So fuck you. Goodbye, Giles." And with that, Morgan stormed out of the shed.

"Morgan—" Giles called after her, but she was already gone.

XVI

IN THE FLURRY OF supernatural events, Morgan and Isobel completely forgot about the homecoming dance.

By the time Morgan arrived back at her house—still fuming after her interaction with Giles—she had about fifteen missed calls from Zach.

Morgan knew the first person she needed to call was Isobel, but she figured she should at least check in with Zach.

"Hey, babe," he answered on the first ring.

"Hey, what's up?"

"Just checking in about tonight," Zach replied. "I was worried about you. Where've you been all afternoon?"

"Around," Morgan sighed. "With Isobel, running errands...you know." She searched for an excuse, but simply came up with: "Gotta get gorgeous for tonight."

"Aw, babe, you know you're already gorgeous," Zach laughed.

"Yeah, well," Morgan replied, getting simultaneously irritated and bored by the inane conversation. "You know how it is."

"Totally."

"Beauty takes work."

"Right."

"Or pain, or...whatever. However the saying goes."

"Well, you're always beautiful to me," Zach reassured her.

Morgan cringed.

"So...about tonight," Morgan started, but faltered. She quickly realized that she had no idea how tonight was supposed to work. She needed to talk to Isobel first of all, find Dani, *deal* with Dani, get stupid Giles out of her head...and then, of course, deal with all the homecoming bullshit. Hair, makeup—shit, a dress. She didn't have a dress.

"...then I figured we could just all head over together," Zach finished.

Morgan realized she hadn't been paying attention to a word he'd been saying.

"Uh...right," she replied warily.

"So that's cool, then?"

"What?"

"We'll just pick you and Isobel up?"

"Oh, right."

"And what about that girl Dani?" Zach asked. "I know you've got your claws out for her right now, but I really think Giles wants to—"

"*Giles*?" Morgan demanded, suddenly enraged.

"Yeah," Zach responded. "Wait, what's up? You two fighting?"

It fucking figures, Morgan thought. Of *course* he would be at the dance—why wouldn't he? Everyone still thought he was just a normal student. Only she knew the truth. And even if Zach had made some sort of deal—which, frankly, Morgan seriously doubted—Giles was probably just messing with her. She tried to reassure herself. That didn't mean that he knew anything about Giles's...what had he called it? His "true form."

"Um...no," Morgan laughed. "No more than usual, you know."

"That's good. You two are like brother and sister sometimes," Zach said. Morgan could hear him smiling on the other end of the line. She felt grossed out.

"I don't know about *that*...but yeah, it's fine." Keep up appearances, Morgan, she reminded herself. "We're good. So he's going with Dani, huh?"

"That's the word on the street."

"Cool. Great."

Morgan felt her jaw clench.

"So we'll pick you up at your house?" Zach asked.

"No..." Morgan trailed off, a plan slowly forming in her mind. "No...Isobel's house. My mom has book club tonight here." At least that part was true, she thought bitterly. No need to drag good old Dr. Firestone into any of this. "We'll all be there. Me, and Isobel, and Dani too. We'll all be there."

"Cool. Can't wait!"

Morgan rolled her eyes.

"Me neither, babe."

"See you then, gorgeous!"

Morgan ended the call and immediately closed her eyes, focusing in on Dani. She could see Dani's image before her perfectly—like before, but with more clarity this time.

"Get the fuck over here," she commanded.

In her mind's eye, Morgan saw Dani stand and nod as if she had no will of her own.

"And if you try anything," Morgan added. "I'll destroy you."

Dani nodded once more.

Morgan opened her eyes. She knew all she had to do was wait. Sighing, she flounced over to her closet and threw open the double doors. Nothing. Worthless. Four years' worth of colorful yet tasteful gowns—proms, homecomings, winter formals, beauty pageants—but absolutely nothing to wear tonight.

What unbelievable bad luck.

XVII

MORGAN APPLIED A FRESH coat of lipstick, unlocked the heavy front door of her house, poured herself a glass of red wine, sat down at the head of the dining room table facing the entryway, and waited.

Morgan tapped her glossy red almond-shaped nails on the newly varnished surface of the table. She could feel Dani approaching.

As soon as Morgan sensed Dani outside the house, she closed her eyes, again focusing on Dani's image in her mind, and warned her:

"Don't try anything."

Morgan heard the steady click-clack of Dani's Target-brand stilettos on the stone pathway leading up to the porch; she glanced down at her own Louboutins and smirked, took a sip of wine, and steeled herself for the interaction to come. Pure confidence, she reminded herself. You've got this.

Moments later, Dani opened the door and let herself into the spacious entryway.

Morgan took another sip of wine and smiled tightly at Dani.

"Morgan," Dani stated, nodding in acknowledgement.

Morgan motioned toward the end of the table.

"Please, sit down."

Dani sat uncomfortably, shifting in the oversized chair.

"Can I get you something to drink?" Morgan

asked, standing and heading over to the bar cart by the entrance to the kitchen without waiting for an answer

"Um, no, thank you," Dani replied.

"I think you're going to want to join me in a glass of wine," Morgan said, filling a crystal goblet with some of the Bordeaux she had opened earlier.

"I don't—" Dani mumbled anxiously.

Morgan sashayed over to Dani and placed the glass in front of her.

"*Drink*," Morgan commanded.

Dani obeyed.

Morgan smiled and returned to her chair at the head of the table.

"Dani," she began. "It seems like we have something of a problem here. I know you feel persecuted—*believe me*, I understand. You're scared. We're all a little freaked out right now. That's normal. What happened is...fucked up, to be honest. There's no other way to look at it. But we have to keep our heads on straight. We can't be turning on each other. And, above all, we *certainly* can't let anyone outside of the group know that there's anything weird going on. Right?"

Dani nodded.

"Right," Morgan continued. "Take another drink."

Dani complied.

"*So.* Here's what we're going to do. Do you have a dress for the dance tonight?"

Dani shook her head.

"Okay. Me neither. That's fine. We're going to head over to Saks and pick up two dresses—"

Dani started to interject, but Morgan held up her

hand.

"My treat. And then we're going to go over to Isobel's house, where our dates will pick us up. *You* will be going with Giles, and you're not going to say one word about it. I know you're not happy about that. I'm not either. But what can you do? We're going to drink some wine—drink, Dani."

Dani took another sip.

"Good. We're going to drink some wine, and dance to some really awful music, and have our photos taken for the goddamn yearbook, and we're going to have our names called for the homecoming court. And everyone will applaud and we'll stand on stage and wave, and smile, and look *so* fucking happy. Because what you'll learn soon enough, Dani, is that that's all anyone cares about. That you *look* so fucking happy."

Morgan paused and took another sip of wine.

"You give a beauty-queen-smile and they get a picture for the yearbook, and everyone feels more comfortable," she continued. "Safe. *That's* the service we do for the people of Golem Creek—the other kids at Honorius High. Our fucking big-toothed-bullshit-empty-eyed smiles make them feel like everything is safe. *We* have those dreams so that *they* can sleep at night. Our smiles maintain the pretense that evil isn't real. And it's bullshit. It's all bullshit. But we do it. Isobel and I have done it for years—you're going to do it *once*. So yeah, it sucks. But you figure out a way to deal. We accept whatever bullshit crowns and flowers or whatever it is that they give us. And we smile. And then after the dance the three of us will come back to my house and we will figure all this out, okay?"

Morgan was pleased with how benevolent she was being. Given her newfound powers, she could literally make Dani do whatever she wanted. Forcing her to enjoy a night of high school revelry seemed like a very small request.

Dani's eyes were wide; she was staring at her feet.

Morgan pursed her lips and began rapping her fingernails on the surface of the table.

"I think you want to take another drink now," Morgan suggested, narrowing her eyes in annoyance.

Dani obeyed.

"Now, is there anything you would like to say?" Morgan asked, taking a sip of her own wine.

Dani narrowed her eyes.

"I don't trust you."

"Okay," Morgan replied.

"And I don't like you," Dani stated flatly.

"That's fine," Morgan said, raising her glass. "I don't like you either. Now, cheers."

XVIII

Morgan had gotten used to acquiring luxury items with suspicious ease and at alarmingly low cost over the past four years. Designer clothes and handbags seemed to simply fall into her lap. A friend of her mother's would drop off a vintage Chanel purse or Hermès scarf, or she would find herself the sole recipient of a miraculous one-day-only 80%-off sale at Saks. Nobody but Isobel knew of Morgan's luck, and Morgan was kind enough to share the spoils of her victories with her best friend. Morgan and Isobel's supposedly unlimited budgets set a dangerous precedent at Honorius High—which, before their ninth-grade debut, was certainly not a school known for its fashionistas. Golem Creek wasn't exactly New York City, after all.

But Morgan had never experienced anything like her shopping trip with Dani that afternoon.

Morgan, with Dani in tow, breezed into Saks Fifth Avenue that afternoon with fifteen minutes to spare and very little patience.

"You're going to fit us into two fabulous gowns, two pairs of shoes, and find us whatever additional accessories we might need," she announced to the mousy saleswoman in the Formal and Eveningwear department. "And you're going to give it to us for free. We're your thousandth customer."

Morgan heard Dani cough behind her.

"*I'm* your thousandth customer. According to the

rules of your contest I get to pick a friend to share this win. And I choose," Morgan glanced over her shoulder and pointed limply at Dani, "I choose her."

"Of course," the saleswoman said in awe. "Of course! How exciting!"

"Right?" Morgan asked, smirking.

"Whatever you want—right away!"

In exactly fifteen minutes, Dani and Morgan were followed out of the store by a coterie of salespeople, all carrying garment bags and boxes to deposit in Morgan's red Mustang.

Once both girls were seated in the car, Dani smiled for the first time that day.

"Okay, Morgan...that was pretty cool."

Morgan adjusted her sunglasses.

"I tipped them all, anyway," she added. "So technically we're not stealing."

By the time Morgan and Dani arrived at Isobel's house some of the tension between them had thawed.

Isobel, however, was a nervous wreck.

"Well? How did things go with Giles?" Isobel demanded before Morgan had even set foot in the door.

Morgan sighed and rolled her eyes beneath her sunglasses.

"Chill, Isobel. Say hi to Dani."

"Hey, Dani," Isobel muttered, chewing on a nail.

"Don't mess up your manicure," Morgan ordered.

Isobel's hand dropped from her mouth.

"Hey!" Isobel cried. "Don't use your...mind control or whatever..." She trailed off, taking a deep breath and unclenching her jaw. "Actually...thanks."

Morgan smiled.

"You're welcome...aren't you going to invite us in?"

"What are you, a vampire now?" Isobel laughed. "Devil's Mistress wasn't enough? Or whatever it is we are."

"You know what I mean."

"Right," Isobel said, standing aside. "I'm flustered. This is all so—I don't know."

"I know. We all do," Morgan said, removing her sunglasses and gesturing toward Dani. "But we've all agreed to get through the event tonight and then try to figure something out afterward."

"But Giles—Giles is going to be here?" Isobel demanded, anxiously running her hands through her hair and leading Morgan and Isobel up the spiral staircase to her bedroom on the second floor.

"Unfortunately, yes," Morgan said tersely.

"And you saw Giles earlier?" Dani asked.

"Yes..." Morgan replied, trailing off.

"So—what?" Isobel demanded. "What's his game? Do we have anything at all to go on?"

"Giles is a liar," Morgan spat. "And an asshole. And..." she paused, trying to think of another insult, but coming up short. "But I don't think he's dangerous. He's being...controlled. Or something. He works for someone else."

"That...*thing*...in the woods?" Dani whispered.

"Yeah."

"So what do you *mean* he's not dangerous?" Isobel demanded. "He works for a monster. The devil, for all we know."

"It's complicated," Morgan sighed. "I'm fucking pissed at him. I'm—in no way am I excusing, or forgiving, his behavior. But..." she trailed off. "We all know, he wasn't the one who—I just think it's more complicated at the moment. We still have a lot to piece together. We can't figure it all out right now. Let's just get through this bullshit tonight and then we'll pick this back up later, okay?"

Isobel and Dani stared at Morgan, incredulous.

"I said, okay?" Morgan repeated.

XIX

THE REST OF THE evening flew by in a haze of Miss Dior perfume and hairspray and setting powder. When the boys arrived at Isobel's doorway it was almost as if no time at all had passed.

Giles was, of course, in human form. Looking even better than usual, Morgan noted—though she wished she hadn't.

Zach looked perfect, as always. Magazine-cover perfect. Boring perfect.

Morgan knew she looked fabulous. Her friends did too. She was particularly proud of their little group this year. Senior year, best for last.

Still, homecoming at Honorius High was about the last place on earth Morgan wanted to go in the midst of a supernatural crisis.

But Morgan had a duty to her classmates. That was her reasoning, anyway. She'd traded so much for the position she now found herself in. Why not grace them with her presence one last time?

And so she did.

The dance was entirely derivative. Dull, as all high school dances are, with the looming sense of potential excitement that never quite manifests and the lingering sense of bitter disappointment.

As predicted, Dani and Isobel were named to homecoming Court—alongside Emma and Cynthia, of course. And Morgan herself was named Homecoming Queen, an honor she wished she appreciated, but which fell immediately flat.

All Morgan wanted to do was go home, get in her pajamas, and talk things out with Isobel and Dani.

She kept herself going with quick swigs from Zach's flask of vanilla Smirnoff.

"Take it easy, babe!" Zach warned her, laughing.

Morgan rolled her eyes.

Eventually, however, the vodka went to her head. Morgan found herself dizzy and slightly sick. As her surroundings started to blur, she excused herself from the dance floor and staggered outside for some fresh air.

To her surprise, Morgan came face-to-face with Giles.

"Are you okay?" Giles asked as Morgan stumbled towards him.

Morgan breathed in the cool air and looked up to the stars to steady her vision. It didn't work.

"I think I'm going to be sick," she muttered, lurching forward.

Giles grabbed her by the shoulders and mumbled a few words in a language Morgan didn't understand.

"What the..." she trailed off.

"Now just take a deep breath," Giles instructed.

Suddenly her head cleared.

"What the hell did you just do?" she asked.

"I told you, I have some control over states of... inebriation," Giles said, releasing his grasp on her shoulders.

"What?" Morgan demanded.

"Satyr stuff...Bacchanals...you know. You really should read up on us. I think you'd find it...well, at least somewhat—"

"Oh my god, shut up," Morgan said, rubbing her eyes.

"Sorry," Giles mumbled. "I just wanted to help."

"I thought that meant you induced it?" Morgan asked irritably.

"What?"

"'States of inebriation.'"

"Oh, right. Usually, yes," Giles continued. "But if it gets out of hand...puts a young woman—or man, as the case may be—in trouble...well, I do what I can to stop that. It's one of the few powers I have left. Besides the glamour, that is."

Morgan was taken aback.

"Well...thank you."

"You're most welcome."

"This doesn't mean we're okay," Morgan warned.

"I know."

"Zach and his goddamn vodka."

"Morgan, there really is something you need to know about—" Giles started, before Zach burst through the door.

"Morgan! Giles! There you two are. I've been worried about you, babe. I should've known. You're such a lightweight."

Morgan chuckled and leaned uneasily into Zach's embrace.

"I'm fine. Just needed a little fresh air."

"I'm headed back inside," Giles muttered, not meeting Morgan's eyes.

Morgan forced a small yawn and leaned into Zach, feigning exhaustion.

"I'm so tired, babe. I think I'm about spent for the

night. Can you drop us off back at home?"

"You, Isobel, and Dani?" Zach asked.

"Yeah, we're going to have a little sleepover...you know, girl stuff."

Morgan thought she saw Zach's eyes flash red for just a second—and in that second she felt her stomach churn, like she might throw up after all. There was something horribly familiar about that flash of red—those eyes—that made Morgan feel profoundly disturbed. She recoiled slightly. Zach grabbed her arm and dug his fingers a little too tightly into the muscle.

"You okay, Morgan?" he demanded.

Morgan saw the flash again—definite this time. Red sparks against empty black pools. Reeling, she suddenly remembered where she'd seen those eyes before. All those nights in the woods...the creature Giles brought her to that first night. The book she signed in her own blood—*his* book, whoever, *whatever* he was.

Morgan suddenly realized what it was that Giles had been trying to tell her about Zach that afternoon.

It had been Zach all along.

Trembling, Morgan raised her eyes to meet Zach's gaze. She couldn't let on that she knew anything. Pure confidence, she reminded herself. Just like before. You're powerful. You've got this.

Morgan relaxed her face into a smile.

"Of course, babe," she laughed. "Just a little too much to drink. You know I can't resist that vanilla vodka you brought along."

Zach grinned.

"Why do you think I brought it?"

XX

MORGAN WAS SHAKING AS they returned inside to the dance. Giles's touch had effectively sobered her up, but she felt dizzy and her hands were trembling. She wanted to get out of there—away from Zach—as quickly as possible.

Isobel and Dani were at the side of the stage chatting with Emma and Cynthia when Morgan approached them.

Beneath the super-precise winged eyeliner and layers of mascara, however, Morgan noticed a strange tinge to both girls' eyes. Something unsettling and familiar. It was just a flash, though, and in an instant it had faded back into wide-eyed insipid glossiness.

Morgan, gritting her teeth through a smile, grabbed Isobel and Dani by the elbows, leading them away.

"Ohmigaaaawwwd, Morgan!" Emma and Cynthia said in unison. "Congratulations!"

"Thanks, girls, love you!" she replied. "Gotta grab these two for a photo op for just a sec, 'kay?"

Emma and Cynthia returned to preening and admiring their own sashes. Morgan's momentary paranoia evaporated, quickly replaced by a pang of jealousy. At least they could enjoy the evening.

"What's up?" Isobel asked, jerking her arm away from Morgan's grasp.

"We've gotta go," Morgan hissed. "*Now.*"

"Everything okay?" Dani said, noticing Morgan's trembling hands.

"No," Morgan said emphatically. "But I can't tell you now. We'll have someone drop us off at my house and talk there. That was always the plan, anyway."

"Can Zach give us a ride?" Isobel asked.

"That's..." Morgan trailed off. "I don't—I'd rather...besides, he's been drinking." Morgan wasn't sure of what to do.

At that moment, Zach and Giles met up with the group.

"Hey ladies, what's going on?" Zach called out. He was obviously intoxicated.

"You know, babe. I really am not feeling so hot—"

"That's too bad, because you look—" Zach began.

"I think we're just going to head back to my place," Morgan interrupted, cutting him off.

"Bummer."

"Yeah, I know."

"You need me to drive?"

"No," Isobel interjected. "I think...you know, I think Mathers can take us."

Morgan had forgotten about Isobel's waste of an on-again/off-again boyfriend Calvin Mather. Head of the science club and debate team, he'd risen in popularity thanks only to Isobel's frankly bizarre sophomore crush on him. After first mishearing his name as "Mathers," they had collectively called him nothing else—despite (and most likely because of) his constant protestations.

He was such a fucking puritan, he certainly hadn't been drinking. It was perfect.

"Yeah," Morgan agreed. "Where is Mathers,

anyway?"

"Probably talking to a teacher or something," Zach chuckled, taking another sip from his flask. "I love the guy, but he's such a loser."

Isobel snorted.

"Hey, man—be cool," Isobel said, holding back laughter.

At that moment, Mathers appeared at Isobel's side.

"M'lady!" he greeted her, bowing.

Zach burst out laughing. Obnoxious.

"See what I mean?"

"What?" Mathers asked quizzically.

"Nothing," Isobel replied, patting him on the head. "Nothing at all. You want to give us a ride to Morgan's? We're over this shit."

"Of course, my dear!" Mathers said. "Anything."

Isobel smiled brightly at Mathers before rolling her eyes in Morgan's direction. Mathers didn't notice—or didn't seem to, anyway.

"Great," Morgan said. "Thank you, Mathers. Let's get out of here."

Morgan immediately headed toward the door, snapping her fingers for Isobel and Dani to follow. She was stopped in her tracks as Zach grabbed her by the arm.

"You sure everything's alright, babe?" he asked, gazing straight into her eyes.

For the first time Morgan realized that *she* was the one completely without power. She couldn't move, couldn't even shift her gaze. She was completely frozen—and she was terrified.

"I...It's...I just..." Morgan stumbled over her

words, attempting to figure out something that would convince him. "I just don't feel good, okay?"

Zach released his grasp, apparently satisfied.

"Okay, then," he said, taking another drink. "I'll see you later, maybe?"

"Later?" Isobel stepped in, grabbing Morgan's hand.

"I think we're all pretty tired," Dani added, putting her arm around Morgan's shoulders.

Morgan, not used to feeling vulnerable, felt her cheeks flush with embarrassment. But she felt safe for the first time all night.

"Well, alright...I'll call you then," Zach said warily.

"Sounds good," Morgan whispered as the three girls turned away and headed to the door, followed shortly by Mathers.

What none of the girls heard as they exited the dance floor was Zach leaning in toward Giles and hissing: "You follow them home *now*. Report back to me later."

XXI

THE RIDE HOME WAS mostly silent. Morgan knew she couldn't confide in her friends with Mathers listening, and Mathers wasn't much of a conversationalist on his own anyway.

By the time they pulled up to Morgan's driveway, barely anyone had said a word. Mathers seemed cheerful, however, so Morgan felt a bit more relaxed.

"Feel better, Morgan!" Mathers called out as the girls proceeded up the winding driveway, Morgan still leaning heavily on Isobel and Dani as if she was just slightly too drunk to walk on her own.

"Thanks, Mathers," Morgan replied, turning around briefly to catch his eye before he rolled up the tinted window of his dark blue jeep and drove off into the night.

As soon as Mathers's car was out of sight, Morgan straightened up.

"We have a lot to catch up on," Morgan stated, slipping her key into the lock on the front door. "And it's...not good."

As soon as Morgan opened the door, however, all three girls stopped dead in their tracks.

There, at the dining room table where Morgan and Dani had sat drinking Bordeaux just hours earlier, were Morgan's mother, Isobel's mother, and Dani's mother. Each woman had a glass of red wine in a crystal goblet in front of them.

"What the..." Morgan trailed off.

"Close the door, Morgan," Dr. Firestone ordered.

This time, Morgan obeyed.

"Girls, please join us," Dr. Gowdie said, gesturing elegantly to the three other seats at the table.

Morgan noticed that Dani's mother didn't say a word.

The three girls moved warily toward the table.

"I'm not...we're..." Morgan began, but her mother interrupted her.

"Morgan, this is an order. *Sit.* "

For the second time that night Morgan felt entirely powerless. She sat down, just as her mother told her to. Isobel and Dani did the same.

XXII

"THIS CONVERSATION HAS BEEN a long time coming," Dr. Firestone began.

"Eighteen years, in fact," Dr. Gowdie added.

"But it's time you girls knew the truth...and, unfortunately, for reasons not completely clear to any of us, frankly, we had to wait until now to reveal it," Dr. Firestone finished.

Both Dr. Firestone and Dr. Gowdie turned toward Dr. Rider, who was nervously sipping her wine.

"Rebecca?" Dr. Firestone asked. "Why don't you take it from here?"

Dr. Rider took another sip of her wine before raising her eyes to meet the three girls.

"As you girls may know...uh...as you, Dani, as you definitely know...I am a history professor at the university here in town specializing in, uh, in witch—in *historical* witchcraft."

Morgan and Isobel exchanged glances. They certainly didn't know that. Dani dropped her gaze to the floor.

"The reason I found myself interested in the subject was...well, Dani," Dr. Rider said, looking uneasily at her daughter, "was because, Dani...I'm a witch."

"We're *all* witches," Dr. Firestone added.

Morgan felt her jaw drop. Isobel burst out in poorly timed laughter.

"It's genetic," Dr. Gowdie added. "We've been

born into the sisterhood. And, therefore, so have you three. You may have noticed some...*changes* recently."

"Changes—powers, etc." Dr. Firestone clarified.

"All perfectly normal for a developing witch," Dr. Gowdie said reassuringly.

"We're terribly sorry we couldn't tell you sooner," Dr. Firestone said, gazing at the three girls with that artificial, all-encompassing therapist's empathy that Morgan so despised. "But you have to understand, we're under certain..."

"Orders," Dr. Gowdie whispered.

"Orders, yes," Dr. Firestone said emphatically. "Orders that prevented us from being completely honest with you girls."

The girls sat in silence for a moment before Dr. Firestone cleared her throat and gave Dr. Rider a pointed look.

"Rebecca, I think you have a bit more to..."

Dr. Rider took another drink and glanced nervously at the girls.

"Yes, right. I assume you girls must have a lot of questions. And we're happy to...you know, we're more than happy to discuss whatever—"

"Well, we all have our specialties," Dr. Gowdie added. "Emotional needs, go to Dr. Firestone. For anything physical, of course, come to me...and as far as our history, that's where Rebecca comes in."

"Right," Dr. Rider nodded. "So...the thing is, girls. In addition to being witches, you are all actually... uh...sisters."

"Excuse me?" Morgan and Isobel demanded in union, leaning forward.

Dani sat stock still, still staring at the ground.

"Uh, yes," Dr. Rider replied. "You were all...sired, shall we say, by the same...entity."

"Holy shit," Morgan whispered.

"Morgan!" Dr. Firestone snapped.

"Excuse me, mom? You drop all this on me and you're going to suddenly have a problem with my cursing?"

"In front of company..." Dr. Firestone began, before trailing off. "You're right, forget it."

"And exactly what 'entity' are you talking about?" Morgan demanded.

"Well," Dr. Firestone said, glancing at Drs. Gowdie and Rider. "Some call him Baphomet...though we're not entirely sure if that's accurate. Mostly he's known as The Creature."

"Right. So. He—what? He waits in the woods for a full moon and then he draws in young women and promises them powers untold if they sign his book?"

"Uh—well, yes," Dr. Rider said nervously. "How...?"

"Because you're all too late. Your goddamn secrecy fucked us. We all signed the book, we all..." Morgan trailed off, unable to finish her sentence.

"We all made the deal," Dani finally spoke up.

The three doctors sat perfectly still, staring at their daughters.

Finally, Dr. Firestone dropped her head into her hands.

"Shit," she mumbled. "Are you kidding me?"

"No," Morgan whispered.

"I told you," Dr. Rider snapped, standing abruptly and storming over to the bar to pour herself another glass of wine. "I told you both. I told you I'd been having those dreams. I knew something was wrong and you didn't listen. You *never* listen."

"I'm sorry, Rebecca," Dr. Firestone quipped, "but it's been a little hard to take you seriously recently with the amount of alcohol you've been putting back."

Dr. Rider turned furiously and narrowed her eyes at Morgan's mother.

"And why, exactly, do you think I started drinking in the first place? I knew this was going to happen...I knew—and Cassandra knew."

Dr. Gowdie shifted in her seat, refusing to make eye contact.

"We've both had the dreams, and I know you have too—you just don't want to talk about it. For a therapist, Catherine, you're seriously in denial."

"Wait, you've been having the dreams too?" Morgan asked.

Dr. Firestone closed her eyes and took a sip of wine.

"Yes," she finally stated.

"We...all have," Dr. Gowdie confirmed.

"But this is all—this is beside the point. Golem Creek was supposed to be a safe place for you girls to grow up without...without making the mistakes that we made. You were supposed to come of age as witches all on your own. Without making any deals, without signing any books, without having to go through all that horrible ordeal. We made a pledge, and we safeguarded this area so that he couldn't recruit—"

"He's not," Morgan said flatly.

"Excuse me?" Dr. Firestone asked, perplexed.

"He has a satyr working for him. Like...a slave or something. It's the satyr who is doing the recruiting."

"A satyr?" Dr. Gowdie demanded. "Here in Golem Creek?"

Isobel and Dani looked at Morgan, confused.

"Morgan, what are you talking about?" Isobel asked.

"He claims he was brought here in 1922—"

"Raymond Clarke," Dr. Rider spat. "All these years later and we're still cleaning up Raymond Clarke's messes."

"And it was this...this *satyr* who recruited all of you?" Dr. Firestone asked.

"Yeah," Morgan muttered.

"When?"

Morgan and Isobel exchanged glances.

"When, Isobel?" Dr. Gowdie repeated insistently.

"Just before ninth grade," Isobel whispered.

Dr. Gowdie put her head in her hands.

"Ninth grade?" Dr. Firestone repeated, incredulous. "Four years ago? You signed the devil's book four whole years ago and I'm just finding out *now*?"

"Well what was I supposed to say, mom? I didn't know anything about this!" Morgan cried. "I didn't know if you'd think I was crazy—hell, I thought maybe I *was* crazy at first. But then I met Isobel... things started going so well for us. It worked out, you know. I just didn't...I didn't think anything of it."

"And you had to continue your meetings in the woods, I'm assuming...to solidify the contract?" Dr. Firestone asked.

"Well, yeah."

"That's bullshit."

"Excuse me?" Morgan asked.

"No, not you—solidifying the contract. You don't have to do that."

"Yeah, I kind of figured that out recently."

"This is exactly what we were trying to protect you from...exactly what..." Morgan noticed that her mother's eyes were welling up with tears.

Dr. Firestone turned to Dani and her mother.

"I...Rebecca, I'm sorry. All this time Cassandra and I...judging you for keeping Dani elsewhere. All the while she was safe and it was...*we* were the ones who had the wool pulled over our eyes."

Dr. Rider shook her head sadly before glancing up at Dani.

"You too?"

Dani nodded.

"When?"

"Just a few days ago."

Dr. Rider closed her eyes and took another drink.

"I knew..." she whispered. "I just knew. I don't know how. I'm so very sorry, Dani."

Dr. Firestone cleared her throat.

"Girls, why don't we take a little break here...I know you've had a long night. If you want to get out of these gowns, take showers, get something to eat...I don't know. Let's just take a break and reconvene in a little bit, okay?"

XXIII

MORGAN, ISOBEL, AND DANI all collapsed on the floor of Morgan's bedroom. Morgan's head was spinning.

"What...the fuck," Morgan whispered, rubbing her eyes.

"This is officially the weirdest night in history," Isobel added.

"Sisters," Morgan exclaimed, her hands still over her eyes. "Sisters!"

"I always hated being an only child," Dani said quietly, almost to herself.

Morgan and Isobel exchanged glances.

"Well you're not anymore," Isobel said, reaching out for Dani's hand.

"You're not mad at me?" Dani asked softly. "About the whole Giles thing?"

Morgan snorted and grabbed Dani's hand as well. "Fuck Giles."

"I think he might be in trouble, though," Isobel said, sighing. "I don't know...I sort of feel bad for the guy."

"Don't," Morgan replied flatly, rolling her eyes. But inside she felt a twinge of regret. She felt bad for him too.

"Hold on," Isobel said suddenly, sitting up. "He's fucking *here*."

Morgan and Dani sat up too.

"What?" Morgan demanded.

Isobel closed her eyes and was silent for a moment,

then nodded her head conclusively.

"He's outside. He's looking for you, Morgan."

At that moment a rock hit Morgan's bedroom window.

Morgan pushed back the curtains and opened the window.

"Get up here, jackass," she hissed into the night.

"Hello to you, too," Giles's voice emanated from the darkness.

"Don't think that just because you helped sober me up earlier that we're suddenly cool. You're a cup of coffee to me—you're nothing. I'm still pissed at you."

"Yeah, I'm getting that."

"Good, now get the fuck up here. We need to talk."

"How exactly?"

"How what?"

"How do you expect me to get up there?"

"I don't know. You're...magic, or whatever. Figure it out."

"I'm a satyr," Giles replied from somewhere in the garden. "Not a...fuck, I don't know. Not a something-with-wings. I can't fly, Morgan."

Giles was obviously irritated. Morgan was too.

"You can climb, can't you?"

"I—" Giles began.

"Stop wasting my time. Figure out a way up here. *Now*," Morgan ordered.

At that moment Morgan heard the front door open and her mother's stiletto heels clicking across the front porch.

"Well, well, well. What do we have here?" Morgan heard Dr. Firestone ask. "An emissary from The

Creature himself?"

"Shit," Morgan whispered, slamming the window closed and turning back to her friends. "They've got him."

XXIV

MORGAN, ISOBEL, AND DANI rushed downstairs in time to see Dr. Firestone dragging Giles into the house by the horns. Isobel and Dani, having never seen Giles in his true form as a satyr, gasped.

"*What the...*" Isobel whispered.

Dr. Firestone dropped Giles roughly on the marble floor of the entryway and, with a quick, vaguely dismissive flourish of her wrist, sent him skidding across the floor into the living room.

"Rebecca, start a fire," Dr. Firestone ordered. "Morgan, find our guest a chair. Cassandra, you know what to do."

Morgan rushed into the dining room, returning with one of the chairs.

With another flick of her wrist, Dr. Firestone lifted Giles into the air and deposited him in the chair.

"Rebecca," Dr. Firestone repeated. "Fire."

Dr. Rider gazed into the empty fireplace for a moment before Morgan saw a tiny flame appear at the center of the stone hearth. The flame, orange at first, flickered before Dr. Rider's ice-blue eyes as she lightly sliced open her palm with the sharply manicured tip of an almond-shaped fingernail. Holding her hand above her goblet, Dr. Rider dripped a few droplets of blood into the remaining wine, spat into it, then tossed the liquid into the flame. The flame leapt up, shimmering green and blue, growing in size until it completely filled the fireplace and nearly spilled out onto the surrounding floor.

Morgan shivered. The fire was cold.

"Satyr," Dr. Firestone snapped, addressing Giles but not looking at him directly. "How long have you been employed by The Creature?"

Morgan, Isobel, and Dani stepped back as Dr. Gowdie moved toward Giles brandishing a scalpel.

Giles, bound to the chair by Dr. Firestone's magic, struggled, but remained in place.

"What's going on?" he demanded.

"Nothing at all, Satyr. Just tell us the truth and everything will be fine," Dr. Firestone replied, gazing into the fire, her back to Giles.

"This won't hurt a bit," Dr. Gowdie assured Giles as, with surgical precision, she sawed into both of the long, curled horns at the back of his skull and inserted her hands into the jagged incisions.

Morgan shuddered and grabbed Isobel's hand as Giles screamed into the blue-green light of the fire.

"Satyr, that's not an answer," Dr. Firestone said testily.

Giles's olive skin was turning pale; it appeared to Morgan that he was struggling to stay conscious.

"Since 1922," he finally whispered.

Dr. Firestone glanced at Dr. Gowdie, who nodded.

"Excellent," Dr. Firestone said. "Now. How long have you been recruiting for him?"

"Only recently," Giles replied. "Only your daughters. And," Giles added, glancing at Morgan, "I didn't want to."

"Oh?" Dr. Firestone asked, uninterested.

"He has my pan pipes. From Raymond Clarke... he—that's how I was traded. He owns me."

Morgan bit her lip and looked down, unable to meet Giles's gaze.

"You could free me—"

Dr. Firestone furrowed her brow and leaned in toward Dr. Gowdie.

"Are you sure this works?"

Dr. Gowdie nodded.

"I'm telling the truth," Giles mumbled.

"Let's get back to that, then. Frankly, I don't care about your sob story," Dr. Firestone said impatiently.

"It was Morgan...at first. That's all. And then he realized..." Giles trailed off, his face ashen. Dr. Gowdie appeared to send some sort of current through his horns, shocking him awake.

"He realized what, Satyr?" Dr. Firestone demanded.

"He realized he needed all three," Giles replied, wincing but seeming to gain a bit more strength.

"For what?" Dr. Firestone asked, moving toward Giles, looking him in the eyes at last. "Why would he *need* them?"

"He wants to open a portal—to release all the magic he has stored beneath Golem Creek. I don't know why the girls are necessary...I'm sorry. I don't."

Dr. Firestone turned from him and crossed her arms over her chest. Morgan could tell she was irritated. She always knew when her mother felt like someone was deliberately keeping information from her—Morgan experienced this same response every week in their therapy sessions.

"Mom—" Morgan interjected, hoping maybe she could get some information out of Giles. But Dr. Firestone held up her hand, silencing Morgan, and turned back to Giles. Leaning in, Dr. Firestone plucked one black hair from Giles's beard, glanced up at Dr. Gowdie and, with a quick nod, tossed the hair into the fire at the exact moment that Dr. Gowdie send another current of energy through Giles's horns, irreversibly cracking them and sending sharp shards of horn flying through the air. Giles screamed in pain before falling limp in the chair, unconscious.

Morgan gasped, lurching forward, but within seconds Giles sat back up again—this time, however, his eyes were flashing blue-green like the fire.

XXV

"Satyr," Dr. Firestone addressed Giles coldly. "*Sing.*"

Morgan, Isobel, and Dani were frozen, awestruck, as the room filled with a peculiar sound. Unnerving but beautiful, it was as if the sound merged with the air and everything was held together in a strange vibration. Like the strains of a drowned cello, or an electric current deep underwater. Sweeping but with a fluttering vibrato. Haunting, somehow horrifying, yet intoxicating.

As the sound grew louder, Morgan felt her entire body begin to vibrate along with it when suddenly, deep within her own mind, she heard a voice— similar to Giles's voice but deeper, familiar yet somehow strange, speaking in a language she didn't know she knew—intone:

> *Through the mighty void the seeds were driven*
> *Of earth, air, ocean, and of liquid fire…*
> *And the young world took solid shape*
> *Then 'gan its crust to harden, and in the deep*
> *Shut Nereus off…*

Before the voice could finish, the ground began to tremble beneath their feet. Dr. Firestone lunged towards Giles, grabbing him by the throat.

"The Murk—are you talking about The Murk?"

Giles stared at her, unblinking.

I speak only of whence I came, the voice replied.

The sound reached a terrifying crescendo as the trembling intensified. Giles was still in a trance, but Morgan could sense that he was coming out of it. In the final moments of the quake, Morgan fell forward toward Giles, who suddenly turned and fixed his unseeing eyes on her. She tried to pull herself away, but couldn't move. She felt the following statement resonate through her body:

Then might you see the wild things of the wood, Morgan Firestone.

Morgan reeled back in terror just as the deafening sound abruptly stopped and the light extinguished from Giles's eyes. Giles gasped for air and lunged forward, crying out:

"There are more. Collecting and harvesting. Others and other places."

"What?" Dr. Firestone cried. "More what?"

But Giles once again went limp, slumped over in the chair. The light of the fire was dimming rapidly. All six women stood in a circle around Giles, shocked and trembling.

"Is he...dead?" Morgan asked softly.

Dr. Firestone sighed, irritated.

"It doesn't matter. We got what we needed," she picked up her goblet and downed the rest of the remaining wine. "Most of it, anyway."

"It does matter," Morgan snapped.

"Excuse me?" her mother demanded.

"He helped us—he helped me earlier, he helped us just now. He could have lied to us but he didn't. I feel...I don't know. I feel bad for him."

"He tricked you—"

"You heard him earlier. He didn't have any free will," Morgan countered.

"He lured you all into a state of submission, of danger, of...of horrors that the three of us," Dr. Firestone gestured to Drs. Rider and Gowdie, "worked our entire adult lives in the hopes of sheltering you from."

"Maybe we didn't need sheltering," Morgan retorted. "What were you really trying to protect us from? Desire? Power?"

"*Morgan*," Dr. Firestone warned.

"Did you ever stop to think that maybe I liked it? Maybe I wanted it?"

"Excuse me?"

"Maybe...maybe I liked being popular. Maybe I liked feeling power over people. Maybe I liked fucking The Creature in the woods. Because you know what? I *did*. And if you're too scared of admitting that, maybe you liked those things too. Fine. But I'm done. I'm done apologizing."

Morgan reached out and took Isobel and Dani's hands.

"We are going to fight this thing together, no matter what it is. But I don't want to blame anyone else for the choices I made, and I don't want to pretend anymore. I want to own the desire that brought us all here together. And I want *him*," Morgan gestured toward Giles, "on our side."

The room was silent.

"Show me how to heal him," Isobel said to her mother. Dr. Gowdie glanced at Dr. Firestone. Both women stood, frozen, watching as their daughters moved, as one, over to Giles's body.

Morgan didn't know what she was doing, but she followed her intuition as she, Isobel, and Dani all raised their hands in a semicircle around Giles. A soft blue light began emanating from their palms and curling around Giles's broken horns. The shards that had flown about the room now floated toward them, locking back in place. Morgan closed her eyes and took a deep breath in, before exhaling, exhausted.

Opening her eyes, Morgan smiled. Giles was stirring, and the horns were intact.

Dr. Firestone smirked, poured herself a glass of wine, and collapsed on the white leather couch.

"You're free, Satyr," she said casually to Giles. "I appreciate your help."

"What?" Morgan demanded.

"Free?" Isobel and Dani asked in unison.

"Free from...?" Giles whispered.

"Free from your bond to The Creature."

"What about his pipes?" Morgan asked.

"They aren't real pipes," Dr. Firestone said, taking a sip of wine. "We had to unleash the music locked away in the most ancient part of his memory—that is, in his horns. It's a tricky spell. Rather, it's a tricky spell to break. He's been controlled by The Creature for some time now. But it worked." Dr. Firestone cast a quick glance at Giles, who, though freed from the magic bonds, was still frozen in the chair from shock. "You're welcome, by the way," she said coldly.

"Uh...thank you?" Giles ventured, still obviously uneasy.

"Now that you're free, you have a chance to prove yourself," Dr. Firestone said, regarding him with a stony look. "I suggest you take it."

"But I thought you didn't care about him?" Morgan asked.

"I don't. And I don't particularly like him. And if you two are going to become a...*thing*, or whatever you kids call it, well, we're going to have to have a *number* of therapy sessions about that, Morgan. Just warning you in advance. Both of you, actually. Satyr, you should probably come along too or start doing individual sessions..." Dr. Firestone trailed off and took another sip of her wine. "Regardless. I do think he should stick around. Might be useful after all."

"I thought you wanted to kill him?" Dani asked, looking back and forth from Dr. Firestone to Dr. Gowdie.

"We just wanted to see if you girls could actually do it...real magic, I mean," Dr. Gowdie said, sitting down next to Dr. Firestone and putting her arm around her shoulders. "Not just dreams or intuition. Work together to do the hard stuff. And you did."

"And you did an impressive job, too," Dr. Firestone added. "Don't you think, Rebecca?"

Morgan looked around, suddenly realizing that both Isobel and Dr. Rider had vanished from the group. They had both wandered back over to the fireplace and were gazing into the dying blue-green flames.

"He's coming," Isobel whispered. "And he's not alone."

FIND OUT WHAT HAPPENS NEXT
IN

THE WITCHES OF GOLEM Creek
BOOK II

HOMECOMING

NADIA XAVIER is an East Coast academic described in *Le Journal de 'Pataphysique* as "our newest, grandest Gradiva." When not teaching literature or French to Earth's next generation of wandering intellectuals, she spends her time practicing conjuration in secret conclave with various weird & occasionally ferocious entities. *Red Hot Hex Magick* is her first novel for Fourth Mansions Press.